FIRE and ICE

Brenna Lyons

FIREBORN
PUBLISHING

FIREBORN PUBLISHING COPYRIGHT STATEMENT

Fire and Ice
Includes:
Magmon's Hunger © 2010/2015 by Brenna Lyons
Magmon's Lover © 2013/2015 by Brenna Lyons
Print ISBN: 978-1-943528-23-3
First Fireborn Publication: October 2015

Cover Artist: Brenna Lyons
Cover design by Katlynne Lyons
Photo Credit: 123rf and Dollar Photo Club
Editor: Kathryn Lively
Logo copyright © 2014 by Fireborn Publishing and
Allison Cassatta
Licensed material is being used for illustrative
purposes only. Any person depicted in the licensed
material is a model.

even those masquerading as legitimate retailers, please let us know at sales@firebornpublishing.com or via the author's personal email.

This book is written in US English.

PUBLISHER

FIREBORN
PUBLISHING

PO Box 5216
Haverhill, MA 01835

MAGMON'S HUNGER

DEDICATION

To Tamer, the one who has melted me, from the first night we danced. To the passion that warms our nights and lights our love.

SECTION ONE
GODS DESCENDING

CHAPTER ONE

"There is one true way to celebrate Magmon's Feast," Jaygin breathed.

Elia laughed at her husband's ploy. "As if it is so difficult to get me to warm your bed?"

He planted a hand on the pillar, nearly brushing her ear with his thumb. Jaygin leaned toward her, already hard. "I never mentioned a bed."

Her question was lost in his kiss. Jaygin's mouth was hot and hard against hers, a passionate man made all the more so by the holiday in question.

Elia didn't protest it. Jaygin was a Furian prince, second in line for the throne. If sounds of their love play escaped the room, no one would dare interrupt them. Nor would the servants dare comment on it or pass rumors in the city about their play.

Not that sex outside the bedroom was particularly noteworthy in the capitol city of Aidalyn. The sexual games of young lords were scandalous, but Jaygin was no longer playing the games, and what he chose to do with his banded wife was fodder for no one's amusement but their own.

They'd only been married a moon, and it wasn't unusual for Jaygin to abandon his desk at midday for no better reason than to carry Elia to their bed. Even so, she'd never seen Jaygin like this. He'd always been a patient lover, slow in teaching her the love arts. He'd always treated her like spun glass that was to be handled with care.

There was nothing careful in what he was hinting...and she loved it. Perhaps the holiday was affecting her, as well.

Jaygin pulled at his clothes, peeling off his tunic and loosening his trousers. She unfastened her bed dress and dropped it on the growing pile, her breathing going ragged at the thought of making love in her sitting room. Jaygin's gaze raked over her body, and he buried his face in her throat, nipping at her, leaving love bites that tingled and throbbed in time with her hammering heart.

Elia closed her eyes, tunneling her fingers in his hair. Jaygin nibbled his way up her throat to her mouth, parting her lips for another searing kiss.

Searing... By Magmon, she was hot. Her skin burned everywhere Jaygin touched her.

It is the summer heat. Magmon's feast was held at the height of the season.

Her body burned in other ways, coming to life for him. Jaygin moaned, lifted her, and thrust inside.

Elia screamed in pleasure, full of his cock, branded by his potent need. Jaygin took her hard and fast, pressing her back into the pillar and lodging himself deep.

He roared in climax, driving her over in the force of his release inside her. She panted in delight, wrapped around him, and loosened her grip on his shoulders.

"Oh, Elia," he breathed. "Take me again."

At her nod, Jaygin hardened inside her.

* * * *

Jaygin came to consciousness slowly, his cock delightfully sensitized. His shoulders and back were tender from the bite of Elia's fingernails.

He smiled at the memories of their loving. They'd shown their devotion to Magmon for half the night, one act of love after another, room to room, until they'd tumbled into bed, still joined and praising the Fire God. They'd practiced the rites of passion until long after the revelers in the street had retired in exhaustion.

Magmon be praised! He had no idea what had come over him. Jaygin had always been gentle in his loving with Elia.

He'd been fortunate enough to encounter Elia as an untried maid. Jaygin had taught her the arts of love and taken her as wife. He'd shed her blood on the night before the bands went on in claim of what was his own, in the traditional manner for a royal taking a virgin to band, as she'd wished it. Waiting for her had been maddening, but so few lords were blessed with the opportunity to prove blood, and Elia was worth the wait.

In all the times he'd loved her, Jaygin had never dreamed of pounding into Elia as he had the night before. And—*Magmon help me!*—he still hungered for her. Jaygin turned to her.

Elia lay in a deep sleep, a light sheet across her hip, her breasts and fiery woman's curls half-uncovered. The invitation was too much for him.

Jaygin eased the sheet away, sliding down the bed and to his belly to lay a lick along her swollen slit. Elia moaned, tipping her hips to him unconsciously.

He dined on her, more avidly as she woke squirmed against him. Elia grasped at his shoulders and then his hair, crying out harshly as she climaxed around his tongue. Her hands loosened, then slid away as he rose up over her.

Elia glanced to the windows, her brow furrowing. "Should you not be away?" she asked in thick voice.

Jaygin eased inside her still-spasming body, forcing back his own release. "My father can manage without me for the day."

CHAPTER TWO

"Mi'lord!"

Jaygin looked up from the reports of heavy rains in Frilan's Notch in surprise. His heart pounded at the sight of his stable master. "What is it, Edlan?"

"Your wife is ill, mi'lord. Selan Senior has been sent for. Will you accompany me?"

Will I? If Elia is ill, no force could stop me.

He rose and bolted for the door without donning his jacket. It was unseemly to travel the streets of Aidalyn without proper dress, as if he was a shiftless lord of the southern reaches, but if Elia needed him, a moment was too long to waste.

Jaygin didn't question Edlan further. It was unlikely that the man knew more than he'd imparted already. The fact that they'd sent for the healer priestess told Jaygin whatever ailed her was no simple cough that steam and mint might ease.

The hectar between his office at the city center and his home at the outer gardens fell away at breakneck speed. He left his horse at the porch and marched inside.

Balrel, the house steward, met him in the foyer, looking harried as Jaygin had never seen him. The servant reached for his jacket, faltered, then pulled his hands back, murmuring his apologies.

"What happened to Elia?" Jaygin demanded, heading for the stairs.

And so quickly. She'd been well that morn, though she'd tarried in bed when he'd risen to start the day. It wasn't the first time she'd done so, and he'd dismissed it. Had he missed some clue as to her state?

Balrel fell into step beside him. "Her ladyship has fainted away twice this morn. The first time, she was in the parlor. A maid saw her fall and called for me to aid them. The second... I was helping her back to bed. I carried Lady Elia up, left her to her maids, and called for Selan Senior. And you, of course," he added hastily.

"Was her stomacher too tight?" Jaygin had thought Elia had more sense than to risk herself to the passing fads of high fashion, but anything was possible. A silly stomacher was preferable to some mysterious malady, at any rate.

Balrel darkened, and his spine stiffened in affront. "I am sure I would not know, mi'lord."

"Of course." He left the steward in the corridor and entered their rooms without knocking. Even if Elia was disrobed for examination, he was her husband and privy to such intimate details of her. Elia was not the spoiled type of woman who hid herself from her husband, thank Magmon.

Elia lay beneath a light quilt, wearing her best bed dress and unnaturally pale.

Magmon! What ails her? She'd been fine the night before. How could her health turn so quickly?

"Mi'lord Furia," Selan Senior greeted him, striding across the room from the hearth she'd been tending.

Was Elia fevering? Was there a fear of chill? Autumn was only starting to nip at the heels of summer, and the house seemed a comfortable temperature to him.

He pushed that question away. There were more important ones to attend to. "What is this illness, priestess?"

She smiled warmly. "It will pass in time and leave no lasting mark. Until then, a maid or steward to steady her would be best."

"But what *is* it?" Why would she not answer him?

"Jaygin?" Elia called out, her dark eyes opening and then seeking him out.

She moved toward sitting, and he rushed to her, pressing a kiss to her forehead and easing her back to the pillows. As if in confirmation that he'd been right, her color waned further.

His heart stuttered in response. "I will care for you," he vowed. "Whatever you require will be provided, Elia."

"Did you tell him, Selan?" There was a note of hurt in Elia's voice that Jaygin wondered at. She'd never been the secretive sort.

"No, mi'lady." The priestess seemed amused by the question. "I thought you might like to do the honors."

Jaygin scowled. "Your stomacher was too tight?" he guessed.

Elia laughed, shaking her head.

"Then, what?" What else would amuse the priestess so?

She blushed, placing a hand over her belly.

Jaygin stared at it, his mind working at an exciting possibility. "A babe? You carry?" Few couples conceived so quickly.

Elia nodded, and he crowed in joy. It was all Jaygin could do not to spin his wife in his arms, but he reminded himself that she was dizzy enough.

The click of the door latch announced Selan Senior's departure. No doubt any further instructions would be relayed to Balrel, on her way to the door.

"I am glad this pleases you," Elia chattered, sounding more herself.

"Of course." Just because it was unusual for a couple to have children so young didn't mean he didn't embrace it. Perhaps having children younger meant he'd be closer to them than his father had been with Jaygin.

But what about Elia? She is losing a young woman's pleasures so soon. Would she hate him for it? "Does it please you?" he countered.

"Very much." A content little smile curled her lips, and she sighed.

Jaygin settled on the mattress beside her, laying a kiss on her lips tenderly. "When will the babe arrive?" he asked. They'd been banded in marriage less than a season, but that left him with a season of possible arrival times, and there was much to prepare.

"The end of winter."

His mind spun, the mental calculations making his heart stutter. Considering the long northern winter, that placed the date of conception—

"You conceived on Magmon's Feast?"

"Or very close to it," she confirmed. "Oh, Jaygin! It is such luck to conceive at the Feast."

He forced his heart rate to ease. There were hundreds of babies conceived in Furia every feast, and there were twenty-nine years until the cen-centenial. Just because the priests had started looking for the He-Atal a year earlier didn't mean their child was the God Vessel. It might not even be this year; the youngest He-Atal had been only twenty-five at presentation. It had never been a member of the royal family before.

"Karliss," Elia breathed, breaking him out of his troubling thoughts.

"Pardon, my love?" Jaygin asked.

"I would like the name Karliss, if I carry a son."

He chuckled at her excitement. "As you wish. My son—if it is a son—will be named Karliss. Remember to choose a name for a daughter, Elia."

She didn't question his offer to let her name their child without hindrance. Elia stroked at her flat belly, her voice wistful. "It will be a son. I know it will."

CHAPTER THREE

"Master Elb! Come quickly."

He turned to the young priest in surprise, noting Ronat's upset. *Perhaps not. It appears to be excitement.* "Yes, Ronat?"

"Selan Senior has sent for you, and she bids you come with all due haste."

Elb rose from the fireside, donning the cowled cloak he wore over his floor-length robes when he had to walk the wintery streets of Aidalyn, Furia's capitol city. He strode into the corridor, glancing to Ronat as the young priest joined him.

"Where are we going?" Elb asked.

"Selan Senior's coach waits. There is no time to prepare your own."

No time? That meant it was urgent. "What is the emergency? Tell me."

"Lord Jaygin's wife is laboring."

"Badly," he surmised. If it was going well, Selan would have no need of him. Elb winced at the idea of them losing a member of the royal family.

The glee in Ronat's voice was impossible to miss. "She fevers, Master."

Elb's heart stuttered at the possibility that the He-Atal was upon them. Every priest and priestess had been watching for the signs for nearly two years, but Elb had never dreamed he would be blessed with the find. "Are the signs right?"

"The fever came suddenly, as labor progressed." He paused for a moment. "It radiates out from the womb."

"Magmon lives," Elb breathed. *Or so we hope.*

The trip to the younger prince's home was a whirlwind, and Lord Jaygin himself met Elb at the door. The prince was tense and pale, and he weaved on his feet at the sight of Elb on his porch.

"Magmon sear it," he choked out. "Elia is dying. Or...my child is?" He looked to Elb for answers the cleric didn't have to give him.

Elb reached for him, guiding Lord Jaygin to a chair. The other man didn't fight him, probably steeling himself for shattering news.

"Perhaps not," Elb soothed the harried young prince.

"Women of a fever—"

"There is another possibility," Elb informed him.

Lord Jaygin looked up at him, a prayer in his eyes. "Tell me."

"There is a possibility...slim, I admit..."

"Master, tell me." His voice took on a cutting edge.

"If your child is touched by Magmon, they may both live and the fever pass with the child."

Lord Jaygin didn't respond to that, so Elb continued. "If he is marked by Magmon's hand, you must let him be trained. It is the will of the Fire God that he do so."

"Give up my son to the priests of Magmon? I would lose my heir to you?" He visibly fumed at the idea.

"Never. He would train in your home until the age of sixteen, then at the temple in Magmalen, but he would still be your son. There would be holidays, as if he attended preparation for the throne in Volcalen."

"He would be a priest, then?" the prince asked, seemingly hoping that would be the case.

"Not a priest." Elb hesitated. He would have to do this carefully. Even lowborn with no hope of better for their sons usually resisted the truth, when it was presented. A prince, facing the possible loss of his heir to Frilan, would balk at what the gods asked. "The cen-centenial approaches."

Lord Jaygin nodded. "In twenty-eight more—" His eyes went wide, and his color dipped to a sickly gray. "He-Atal? My son is to be the He-Atal?"

Elb sighed. "If the fever is Magmon's fire, he is. Only time will answer that question. I cannot, until the babe emerges into the world."

The prince squeezed his eyes shut. "I pray he is. I pray it, because it means he may survive this night."

"As do I," Elb assured him. After giving Lord Jaygin hope of it, it would be a disaster to lose either Lady Elia or the child she carried. "May I see them?"

The prince nodded wearily, pushing to his feet. "This way, Master Elb."

The princess was abed. Her thin bed dress was plastered to her sweat-coated skin, and she was crimson from head to foot. Servants rubbed her down with cloths, and the windows were thrown open to the winter air.

Elb sought out Selan's panicked face. "You let them do this?" he demanded. Was she mad? If the babe was the He-Atal, he would be consumed by Magmon's fire and in need of a warm welcome.

"I could not stop them," she protested.

He nodded, waving a servant away from Lady Elia's side. He motioned the girl toward the windows. "Dragon's fire, close them," he ordered.

The servant looked at Lord Jaygin, visibly torn between the orders of the clergy and those of her liege and his advisors in such matters.

"Close them," the prince rasped. "Do whatever Master Elb orders. Magmon sear my soul if I am wrong."

"And mine," Elb answered.

Lady Elia muttered words too low to hear. Elb sank to the mattress next to her, lowering his ear to within a hand's width of her mouth. He gasped in surprise at her recitation of the birth of Magmon in ancient Seh, the gods' language. No one but the priests and priestesses of Magmon and the priestesses of Frilan spoke Seh. No one else even had the opportunity to learn it, save the Ician and the He-Atal.

He laid a hand on her burning forehead, matching her cadence.

"Magmon's fire," Selan cursed. "Do not stop, Master Elb. The babe is coming fast."

Lady Elia's voice broke, coming in gasps and panted breaths, skipping phrases and matching Elb's recitation when she picked up again.

"What is she saying?" Lord Jaygin asked.

Selan answered, a sure sign that she recognized Elb couldn't risk interrupting the chant to do so. "It is the birth song of Magmon."

The chill of the room cut through Elb's concentration. *Magmon sear it!* The He-Atal couldn't be brought forth into this icy room.

He snapped the fingers of his free hand for attention. He pointed to the main hearth and motioned upward, not missing a beat in the recitation. He looped through smoothly and began the song again, his voice growing stronger.

"Bonfires," Selan barked. "Light them now. Use wax and oil to burn it hot and fast, and keep it fed."

"What?" Lord Jaygin shouted.

"The babe must be warm enough. The shock of this could kill him, after the furnace of the womb."

"Light them. Dragon's breath, light the fires!"

Servants scattered, and shouts and confusion followed. Elb ignored them, repeating the song over and over, his voice going hoarse.

The heat in the room rose to a scorching high. Elb dropped his cloak and drew open the fasteners on his robes. It was like the days he'd spent in Magmalen, and he wished he had a native wrap or a priest's trousers instead of his robes.

The princess launched up, crying out in pain, and Elb held her to his chest, shouting the song in a panic. By the Fire God, he prayed he'd done well in preparing the He-Atal's reception. The gods alone knew what would happen if he'd failed them.

"He's coming," Selan cried out. "A few moments more."

Those moments seemed endless. Selan screamed in pain, and Elb looked to her in surprise, faltering in the song and then matching Lady Elia again. The priestess wasted no time; she took a folded cloth from the pile and used it to grasp the babe's protruding shoulder. She rocked the babe, aiding him in his descent.

At last, the princess crumpled against him, her breathing easing, her skin cooling beneath his hands.

Elb felt for her pulse, sighing in relief that it was strong and steady.

"Lord Jaygin," he called.

The prince appeared at his side. "Is she—"

Elb grasped his hand and pulled Lord Jaygin to the mattress behind his wife, guiding her into his arms. "Care for your wife, mi'lord. I must see to the child."

He slipped past the young royal couple, turning to Selan. His first look at the babe nearly stopped his heard. Wrapped in a nursery quilt and the room akin to an oven, he was still shivering, his lips blue. The young princeling cried weakly and without tears.

The priestess looked to Elb for help, tears rolling down her cheeks. No doubt, she blamed herself for the babe's condition.

"Screen the fireplace," he ordered, at a loss for a better idea. He'd never heard of a He-Atal thus afflicted. Perhaps it was the Aidalyn weather. Perhaps it was the cold during labor. Perhaps Magmon's fire burned hotter at the babe than it had his predecessors. There was no way to know.

That time, the servants didn't question him. The screen scraped against the hearth and thumped into place.

Elb stripped his robes off and dropped them over the foot of the bed, so he stood only in his male covering. He took the babe from Selan's hands and settled before the screen, cradling the babe on his crossed knees. The heat seared Elb, reddening his bare skin, but the babe reached out toward it, sighing. His hand mere finger-widths from the screen, he settled to sleep, his color evening out to a healthy hue.

Lord Jaygin knelt to his side, peeling back the quilt to stare at the mark of Magmon's hand on his son's shoulder. For a moment, he was silent and still.

"Is Lady Elia well?" Elb asked, hoping for a positive response.

"Very well," he breathed. "It is true." The prince dragged his gaze to the roaring fire. "But...must it always be like this?"

Lying to him was impossible. If Lord Jaygin set his mind to it, he could search out records of what comforts the former He-Atal had been afforded by the Furian government. Soldiers and financial comforts were all that had been requested of them, in the past. Large amounts of heating fuel and the men to tend it would have been noted.

"I do not know," he admitted. "I imagine not, but I have never heard of a He-Atal so far afflicted of Magmon's fire at birth. Aidalyn may be too cold for his blood."

"What does he require? My son will have whatever it is," Lord Jaygin vowed.

"Magmalen, until he can cool himself. Then...a temperate border town would be best. Temperara or Frilan's Notch," he suggested.

"The family has an estate in Frilan's Notch. But how do we get him there?"

Elb considered that. "A medical coach. They already have stoves installed. With half the cots removed, replaced with a bed, we could transport you all in comfort."

His mind spun in plans. The king would have to be contacted immediately. They would need a company of soldiers to guard them, as they moved. A royal chef and kitchen coach would have to accompany them. Not to mention, they would need several lories of wood, to be replenished at forts on the way.

Lord Jaygin sighed in seeming relief, his shoulders slumping in the release of tension. "Thank Magmon," he whispered.

Elb stared at him, his mind working at the prince's logic slowly. "The He-Atal needs his family, mi'lord. It is the way of things." Even when the birth family rejected the idea of raising the God Vessel, the priests arranged for an adoptive family to train the He-Atal in a loving home.

Lord Jaygin removed his tunic, revealing a chest glistening in sweat. "May I hold my son?"

"Of course." The bonding of family was something no priest of Magmon worth his name would stand in the way of.

The prince reached for the sleeping infant.

"Do not touch Magmon's hand," Selan instructed.

Elb noted the hand she held in a pan of water and the pain on her face. "You were burned at the birth?"

She nodded, closing her eyes. "A brand of Magmon's hand. I will have need of the Frial ice lotion for quite some time."

He managed a weak smile. "I will send Ronat for it. You are blessed, Selan Senior. In your concern for the He-Atal, you felt his fire as few will. Wear it with pride, my sister."

"When the pain recedes," she joked. "I will be most happy to recount the tale of our glorious Lord's birth, then."

Lord Jaygin lifted his son from Elb's lap gently, offering the babe the heat of the fire to soothe him as nothing else would.

"What is your son's name, mi'lord?" Elb asked.

"Karliss. Elia and I spoke at length about it. His name is Karliss."

SECTION TWO
TRAINING THE FIRE GOD

CHAPTER FOUR

Karliss pulled at his tunic, miserably hot in the southern clime.

"Haven't you dressed appropriately yet?" Master Elb asked, seemingly amused.

Karliss turned to him, uncertain if his burning cheeks were due to the furnace-like heat of the rooms or embarrassment. Either was possible. "How *should* I dress?" he grumbled. He was playing the petulant child, and he knew it. One should not speak to one of Magmon's priests in such a manner, but this heat was untenable.

"What feels right to you?"

Since Elb was shirtless, Karliss stripped off his tunic, sighing in relief. He used the fabric to dry his sweat-coated chest and back.

Master Elb arched an eyebrow. "Cool enough?" he inquired.

A rebellious streak reared up in Karliss, the temper his father had warned him many times he should control better. "Magmon sear it, man! You know I am not." He sat on the edge of the wide mattress and pulled off his boots and socks. He stood again, meeting the high priest's gaze as he peeled off his light trousers.

That was better, but the urge to strip to his gods'-made form was strong and hard to ignore. What would Master Elb do, if Karliss dared such a bold and probably sacrilegious move in the high temple? A nagging voice in the back of his mind dared Karliss to try it and find out.

The worst they can do is send me Frilan's Notch where it is temperate or Volcalen where it is cold. At the moment, cold sounded better than hot.

The cleric sighed. "I can see no one has told you the mores of the temple, Lord Karliss. When you leave the upper reaches of the temple, you will want to wear a waist wrap as the natives wear. When you roam the rooftop, the two floors below it, and all the bathing rooms, at any level, dress as you will, even to nudity, if that suits you. For swimming, at least, you will want to be nude."

"Swimming?" Magmon, but he loved swimming.

"The pond and gardens are yours. Everything on the rooftop level is your own."

Karliss hesitated only a moment. "May I swim now?" Perhaps it would make this heat tolerable until he managed to acclimate himself to it.

"Any time you are not in class, you may spend your time however you wish. But be mindful of the bells that announce meals. A growing young man needs his food, as well as his exercise."

He bristled at the note of condescension in that. In a move of challenge, Karliss pushed his underclothes away and strode out of his rooms without a backward glance to note Master Elb's reaction to it. The cleric didn't voice a reply, nor did he follow Karliss.

There were three paths. One stone path led to the stairs down into the temple, he knew. He followed the unlined path, enjoying the cool soil beneath his feet. If he followed it out and didn't find the pond, he would retrace his steps and try the other.

He'd chosen well. Karliss thanked Magmon for it from the top of the marble stairs that led into the manmade swimming pond. That small religious observance taken care of, he dove in and cut cleanly through the cool water. Refreshed by a few lengths, Karliss lounged on the stairs, half in the water, his eyes closed.

A hand on his shoulder was Karliss's first indication that he wasn't alone. He turned in a panic, meeting the gaze of a young woman not much older than himself. She had dark hair and eyes.

His breath caught in his lungs. She was nude, save the waist wrap the native men wore. Karliss had no clue what it meant. All the priestesses he'd met so far had worn a longer wrap that covered their breasts, as well as their feminine core.

"Who are you?" he managed to ask. "Master Elb said this garden was my own." Was it a communal garden, as the bathing pools were communal?

She smiled. "I am Alina, a priestess concubine."

He hardened at that. Karliss had heard of priestess concubines, but he'd thought they were a tease tale boys told each other. Unlike the healer priestesses who offered service in the medical and midwifery arts and the book priestesses who offered service in teaching children from poor families, the priestess concubines served the men who lived in the temples sexually.

If the stories are sound. There was no guarantee they were.

If they were, did their service extend to Karliss? He was a male within the temple, though he was a man only in name. He wouldn't be permitted to play the sexual games of polite society for another four years.

Surely, they couldn't intend to make him wait that long. It would be cruel to surround him with priestess concubines and deny him use of them.

Who ever said the world was kind?

Alina waited for his answer patiently, though she'd asked no question of him.

Perhaps I should ask one of her. "Have you come to serve me?" His voice didn't crack, by Magmon's grace alone.

He'd hungered for women for a year, but it was unseemly to—

Walk nude in the sunlight. Wear nothing but a wrap in public. Have sex before the age of twenty.

Perhaps it was allowable for him to share in the service of the priestess concubines, after all.

Alina's smile widened. "We came to rub a lotion into your skin, so you will not burn in Magmalen's sun. Once you tan, you will not need it."

His heart sank. Apparently, he wasn't permitted to indulge himself with them.

The rest of the comments filtered in slowly. "We?" Karliss looked around, sighting the other two priestess concubines. His arousal was nearly blinding in its intensity. This was going to be torture.

Alina's voice came from next to his ear. "Of course, if you are interested in our company, one or more of us might choose to cool your fire."

"Yes." Karliss needed cooling. The fire in his blood was worse than he'd ever felt it. "I am interested." He prayed Master Elb wouldn't punish him later for it...or the priestesses for gifting him. *If he punishes me, it will be worth it.*

She stood, unfastened her wrap, and let it fall to her ankles. Karliss didn't look at the others. Alina had his full attention. His mouth went dry, and he licked his lips, drawing in the scent of her body, starved for something he couldn't put a name to.

The first stroke of lotion came from behind. Karliss hissed out his breath at the warmed lotion spreading over him.

"It is to your liking, Lord Karliss?" the one behind him asked.

The one to his left answered before he could. "His cock says it is, Zinia."

Karliss directed his attention to her, taking in the red-gold hair that marked her as a native of the northern border with Frilan. He moaned as she started rubbing the lotion into his chest.

Alina joined in. In moments, Karliss was caught between torment and bliss, three pairs of feminine hands stroking over his body, naked flesh touching naked flesh.

The red-gold one massaged the lotion into his face and neck, and Karliss itched to kiss her as he'd kissed the maids and visitors to his parents' home. "What is your name?" he asked.

"Lurai, mi'lord."

"What are—" He gasped at Alina's hands trailing down his chest. "What are the priestess concubines permitted to...do with me, Lurai?" He'd take any pleasure they'd give him, even if they couldn't chance issue with him.

Zinia giggled and then quieted at a sound of warning from Alina. Karliss felt his temper spike at that. She was laughing at him.

True, I am untried, and she is experienced, but being laughed at by a servant—

"Zinia, leave us," Alina ordered.

The priestess rose and walked away without a protest.

Still stung, Karliss considered pushing the other two away. *If they think me a child to be—*

Lurai urged his chin up, teasing her lips back and forth over his. That quickly, his anger was forgotten and his arousal returned.

Alina moved to his back, wrapping her arms around him to spread the lotion, her breasts snug to his body in invitation.

This close, Lurai's eyes beckoned, drawing him in for another kiss.

"Does my body please you, Lord Karliss?" she asked.

Mindful of Alina, he answered as not to alienate either woman. "You both please me." It was true, but he wanted Lurai. He wanted all of her he could have.

Alina's voice warmed his ear. "You want Lurai more." She spoke as if they shared a secret. "Tell her the truth, Lord Karliss."

"Yes, I do want you more, Lurai. I want you first. What are we permitted to—"

Alina nipped at his ear. "There is no permission in Magmon's temple, mi'lord. You want us and ask our agreement. We choose whether or not to gift you with our acceptance."

"And will you?" he asked. "Both of you? Or must I choose between you?" He would choose Lurai, if it came to a choice, but he'd heard priestess concubines were open to sexual experimentation, sharing of partners, and all manner of sexual kink that even the most adventurous young lords never managed to convince a noblewoman of.

"Please Lurai. If you still wish my company, I may gift it."

Karliss nodded, brushing his lips against Lurai's as she'd done to him. She placed her hands on his cheeks, cocking her head to her right. Her lips parted against his, and Karliss surged inside.

The priestess let him lead from there. Karliss touched and tested, learning the feel of a woman's body without layers of clothing between them. He urged her closer by a grip on her buttocks, and Lurai straddled his legs.

Their kisses became more fevered. Lurai gasped, arching against him, brushing her feminine curls over the sensitive head of his cock. He thrust his hips up; she moved with him so that Karliss hit his mark.

Lurai settled over him, encasing most of his length inside her. He cried out, shocked by the intensity of sensation.

"Slowly," Alina whispered, her hands spreading lotion into his hips. "Just feel her body surrounding you."

The drumming of need assaulting his nerves demanded more, and he thrust up again. Lurai moaned, her beautiful gray eyes closing in pleasure. The fire inside him flared at that, and she gasped as if she could feel it.

"Control the fire," Alina counseled. "Use it."

But Lurai's hips were circling, driving him mad. His muscles trembled in restraint. Surely, if he loosed himself on her, he'd hurt her. Still—

"Deeper," he rasped. "I need to have all of you."

Lurai's eyes opened, and her smile lit them. "You need to be lord this time."

That confused him. "I *am* a lord. I am a Furian prince."

"You are my only lord. Move with me."

She arched her back, easing her weight onto the marble stairs. Karliss turned and pivoted with her, laying out with the weight of his upper body on his arms and his legs between hers.

He surged into her, groaning at the feeling of his sac nestled to her slick body. Alina rubbed lotion into his exposed buttocks, and he shivered in delight.

His tenuous control snapped with a nearly audible crack, spurring him on as if it were a whip laid to his sensitized backside. The rest was a blur of motion and sound...scent and touch.

Climax roared through him, a thousand times more powerful than any he'd given himself. Karliss was certain he was making sound—screaming or perhaps shouting, but he couldn't hear himself.

The next coherent moment for him found Karliss holding tightly to Lurai, his face buried in her throat, panting. "Magmon lives, what was that?" he gasped out. His throat protested the use, abruptly raw and heated, as if he fevered.

One of Lurai's hands stroked through his hair in a soothing motion. Alina's continued with the lotion massage, working up the inside of his legs toward his sac.

His arousal beat at him, bringing his cock back up, heating his blood. The wicked fingers stroked at his sac, kneading them until they hardened again.

"Alina," he begged.

"Turn to me."

Karliss eased out of Lurai, turning to his back.

Alina knelt between his ankles, massaging the lotion up the front of his legs. He tipped his hips up, pleading for her body. She took her time, touching him, stroking his skin, her gaze locked on his.

"Magmon sear your soul," he cursed her. "Come to me or leave me, but stop this!"

She nodded to Lurai.

Karliss looked around, just as the northerner kissed him. He grasped her head, kissing her deeply, ready to take her again, if she were the one willing.

The mouth closing around his cock scattered his tenuous hold on conscious thought. Karliss bowed his back, forcing himself further into Alina's mouth, shouting into Lurai's.

Then they were both moving, Alina up and down his length, Lurai in and out of his mouth, twisting to press her bare breasts to his chest.

Magmon, yes. Oh, Magmon, yes. It was the only coherent thought left to him. He wanted this. He'd wanted the upstairs maid at his parents' home to do this for him, but she'd feared his father's displeasure too much to oblige him.

Alina and Lurai feared nothing. The twin mouths engulfing him weren't going to stop until he was utterly spent.

As if in confirmation of that, Alina took him to the root...and stayed. Karliss thrashed beneath them, moving one hand from Lurai's head to Alina's. One part of his mind urged him to pull Alina back before he went mad. Another recognized the coming of another powerful climax. That part won out, and he pulled them both closer.

His seed coursed out, and his entire body started to spasm. Lurai pulled back, breathing hard, pillowing her hand under his head as if to keep him from striking the marble. Karliss vented a scream into the air, releasing the last of his seed. He collapsed to the step, boneless. His eyes slid shut.

Lurai eased away from him, and Alina's mouth retreated. She covered the last of him with lotion, laying a gentle kiss on his belly.

He was too tired to hiss in displeasure, too tired to open his eyes. Sleep took him, covering him in darkness and silence.

* * * *

Alina smiled at the boy, the God Vessel, the He-Atal. He lay on the step, lost to sleep in the aftermath of his release of passion. In years to come, he would learn to harness the Fire God's hunger. For now, he was a child, clumsily managing the same.

She stroked a hand through his ember-colored hair, holding back a laugh as he moaned and moved against her as if he were a kitten.

"Should we call for the priests?" Lurai asked. "Should we move Lord Karliss to his bed?"

"No. Let him sleep." She glanced at the pond nervously. "But watch him."

"Of course, if he stays here."

The horror in Lurai's voice was more than appropriate. It was too close to the mark to lose the He-Atal to any threat or accident.

Alina rose, donning her wrap. "I will report to the Concubine Senior and Master Elb. A priest will relieve you shortly." She cast a look of warning at her counterpart. "If he wakes before the priest arrives, soothe him, but do not gift him your body again today."

Something about his reaction to his second climax bothered her. It had been intense...much more intense than they'd been told to expect.

Lurai blushed, then nodded her agreement. Certain that the young concubine knew her duty, Alina stood and strolled to the floor below.

She was a few footsteps from Adria Senior's office when the older woman's voice reached her.

"Alina? Would you join us?" Adria's voice was tense, a clear condemnation of something, but what was beyond Alina's ability to comprehend. She turned with a nod, following Adria to the High Priest's office.

Her confusion dissipated at the sight of Zinia, a cocky smile twisting her full lips. Alina's hand fisted, and she resisted the urge to let it fly.

"Zinia claims you dismissed her," Master Elb stated in a clipped tone that warned she was in danger of being dismissed from the temple entirely for it.

"I did." *With good reason, but I must be patient until they know that reason. They will believe Zinia until proven wrong in doing so.*

Zinia crossed her arms under her breasts. "You wanted to be his first," she accused.

Alina managed a tight smile. "I was not his first."

Zinia's jaw dropped.

"He chose Lurai for his first. I urged him to it when I saw his interest in her. And you—" Alina reined in her fury, calling on the calm Magmon's priests taught.

"Would it not have frightened Lord Karliss, you would have tasted the back of my hand instead of being ordered away."

"I? I only—"

"You *laughed* at him."

"I did not!" Zinia protested. "I only meant to—"

"You laughed at him. No matter what you meant, you did. You were behind him, Zinia. You could not see his anger and hurt at it, but I could."

She choked, pressing her hands to her mouth. It was good that Zinia understood her offense, but Alina wasn't satisfied with it.

"I could not allow it. I would not have allowed his first memories to be marred by your unfeeling and unthinking response."

Adria stepped between them, motioning Zinia toward the corridor. "In my office," she ordered. By the look on her face, Zinia would face at least reassignment to another temple. At most, she might be dismissed from service altogether.

The young priestess fled. There was a tense moment of silence in her wake.

Then the high priest spoke. "Lord Karliss had a memorable first experience?"

"He struggles with the god's hunger, but he enjoyed the experience. A priest should be sent to relieve Lurai as soon as possible."

Elb and Adria locked gazes, then looked to her as if demanding an answer.

"Lord Karliss was exhausted. We thought it best not to move him and risk the shock of him waking somewhere other than where he gave in to sleep."

"Agreed," Adria stated.

"Since he lay at the pond, we dared not leave him. I have instructed Lurai not to gift him again, but it would be best if he was not aroused by the sight of another priestess so soon."

Master Elb nodded. "See to it, Adria Senior."

She hurried away.

Alina bowed, believing she was to be dismissed as well.

"A moment, Alina," the high priest called out.

She met his gaze, holding her ground as the door closed behind Adria.

Master Elb seemed to consider her. "You urged Lord Karliss to another?"

"He wanted Lurai. He wanted us both, but he wanted her more."

"Did he have you, as well?" he asked.

Alina straightened. "My mouth," she admitted. "His hunger is fierce."

"Come here."

She went to him, allowing the high priest to guide her to the edge of his desk. He spread her knees, exposing her slick seam to the room air.

"You wanted more." He didn't question it.

"Yes, I wanted all of him, but the He-Atal must learn to control the hunger."

Master Elb's fingers teased inside her seam. "You still want him."

"His heat calls," she gasped.

"Remove my wrap."

She did so, knowing what he intended. The high priest didn't ask and wait for her response, but she didn't want him to act the part of priest seeking gift of a concubine. His wrap fell.

Before her next breath, he was inside her, thrusting hard and deep but still slower than Lord Karliss had. She vented her pleasure to any who might hear them. Not that it would be frowned upon. The deepest devotions to Magmon were shown in such a fashion.

"Lord Karliss left you wanting," he breathed into her ear, "but he is young and learning."

"Will you do this every time he leaves me wanting?" she teased him.

"And more." It was an empty promise, she knew. It was loveplay at its finest.

Master Elb captured her mouth in an involved kiss. He broke away on a low moan. "I taste him in you. Oh, Mag—"

Someone pounded hard on the door, one of the few doors in the temple, startling her.

"Master Elb, we need you!"

Alina was abruptly empty, watching the high priest sprint for the door without donning his wrap.

* * * *

Karliss stretched, grimacing at the odd sensation of hot stone beneath him. He turned, grasping at the edge of the step as he slid off. The lower step caught him, but he was abruptly on his ass and above his waist in cool water.

"Lord Karliss," a man called out. "Are you well?"

He nodded, waving the priest away blearily.

Nothing made sense. Where was he?

The pond. The marble stairs.

Why am I here?

I fell asleep. I was swimming and...

And what? What happened to me?

Memories of the priestesses assaulted him. Karliss doubled over, sweating, shivering. He laid his cheek on his crossed arms, dizzy...weak.

"Lord Karliss!"

An icy hand touched his shoulder and then pulled back. Karliss tensed, swallowing down a cry of pain.

The sensation subsided slowly. Karliss's fingers, gripping the stone as if trying to scratch furrows in it, loosened. His muscles went lax, and he slipped further into the water.

Hands grasped him under the arms and hauled him onto the grass. In the next instant, Karliss was cradled to a broad chest, carried to a bed and settled upon it.

Quilts covered him and were tucked tight around him. The heat brought sleep...dreamless sleep.

* * * *

"What is it?" Elb was already running for the stairs. There was no question that it was Karliss.

"A fever...very sudden."

"He woke?"

Jeru nodded. "Disoriented, but otherwise fine. Then it struck."

"What actions have you taken?"

"He is in his bed with all the quilts from his cabinet."

"Good." If his youth was any indication, Karliss would require as much heat as they could generate until the fever broke. They might even have to build fires in his rooms.

They raced into the sunlight, to Karliss's room, and inside.

The prince thrashed beneath the quilts, sweat-soaked. Elb sat next to him, touching the boy's burning skin.

"What caused this?" he pleaded with no one in particular.

"What can I do?" Alina asked from the doorway.

Karliss stilled, his face turning her direction though his eyes remained shut.

Elb put a hand out to her. "Come here."

Alina appeared at his side. Elb stood and stripped her wrap off, letting it fall. Her breaths were quick and uneven, a sure sign that she was still aroused.

Good.

He pulled the quilts back, baring Karliss. Elb guided Alina to the mattress.

"I do not understand. I thought—"

"When he develops control. Take him, Alina."

She mounted the bed and straddled Karliss, taking him in with a gasp. Karliss grasped her hips, thrusting hard into her. He climaxed in moments...then resumed.

Elb looked to Jeru. "Assemble the priestess concubines," he ordered. "They will take him in turn until he runs the course of Magmon's fire."

"Yes, Master Elb." The young priest bolted away.

Alina cried out wildly, and Karliss followed. He rested only a moment and then started again, a nearly desperate pace.

At his next climax, Jeru pried the prince's hands from Alina's hips, and Elb pulled her away. Karliss fought the priest, leaving little room for the next priestess to take her place and still his fight.

Elb took a cloth from Adria's hand, mopping the seed from Alina's thighs. The young concubine moaned, pressing to his body.

"Pleasure or pain?" he whispered.

"Is it sacrilege to hope he suffers this long enough to come to me again?"

Elb watched Karliss driving into the second priestess. He-Atal had required feasts of love before, but never with this intensity. "At this rate...it may."

CHAPTER FIVE

Jaygin entered Magmon's temple, stiffening in the deluge of memories.

They'd spent Karliss's first two years here. It had been a hard time for them. Elia had never been comfortable in the lady's wrap, all the less so in the waist wrap and nursing vest they'd provided for Karliss's first year and a half. Their quarters hadn't been private enough for her, and their passion had suffered as a result. It had only recovered upon their move to Frilan's Notch. Even now, though she missed Karliss desperately, Elia refused to visit Magmalen to see him.

Jaygin couldn't name what had sent him here, why waiting for the holidays to see his older son was intolerable to him. He tried to convince himself that it was just the jitters of a child leaving home for the first time, but it knew that for a lie.

The memories of the toddler Karliss plagued him.

His son had only accepted the northern summer style of clothing until the age of one. The following year had consisted of him learning control over his temperature. When Karliss had rejected the heavy clothing, the priests had tried to introduce the native waist wrap or trousers, but Karliss would have none of it. Within moments of being dressed for the day, the child would be naked, running from communal baths to gardens, offices to sleeping quarters.

Always, the priests and priestesses found his boundless energy a delight, a sign of Magmon's fire within him. But Karliss had known no propriety. He'd charged in on men and women in any state of undress or intimacy.

Worse, there had been no counseling him. At any attempt to do so, the priests had made it clear that the He-Atal *had* no boundaries within Magmon's temple. They'd argued that Karliss's interest in body and sexuality must not be stifled or discouraged.

When they'd moved to Frilan's Notch, things had improved little. Though the colder climate had convinced Karliss to wear clothing...grudgingly, the hovering priests had made certain Karliss was offered little instruction in the social mores concerning proper dress and sexual limits within the household. It was all Jaygin and Elia had been able to manage to teach him the proper social graces for company without interference.

And the last year— Jaygin bit back a groan at that.

Magmon, but it had been difficult to force the priests to retreat. When they'd learned Karliss was fighting off Magmon's hunger, they'd tried to demand the He-Atal return to them to begin his instruction. Only Elb's word that their son would remain at home until sixteen had circumvented a formal appeal to his father on the matter.

Not that having Karliss at home hadn't been stressful enough. The battle to keep Karliss from maids' beds had only been rivaled by discouraging noblewomen from his.

That is why I came to Magmalen. I know what my son is going to become. I pray to Magmon that he has not of yet.

"Lord Jaygin," Elb called to him.

Jaygin wasn't certain why he bothered with the title, save the veneer of propriety. Over the sixteen years he'd been watching over Karliss, Master Elb had become Elb to him, and Lord Jaygin had become Jaygin to the priest.

The high priest's smile was strained, a sure sign that Jaygin was not a welcome sight.

A pity. My son is within, and I have a right to see him, as I would if I visited him at Volcalen. "Elb," he returned. "I have come to see my son."

"Of course." He glanced at the windows, marking time as Jaygin had learned to in the temple. "Lord Karliss will be in the library with Master Puaul." Elb turned and led the way, though Jaygin remembered the way well enough.

Sweat ran down Jaygin's back, but he refused to remove his tunic and boots as he had when he'd lived within these walls. It was two floors up to the library, and the heat was oppressive by the time they reached it, searing his lungs.

"You could remove your tunic," Elb suggested gently.

"No. Those days are past."

Silence fell between them for a hand of steps, but there was so much Jaygin wanted to know, he could not remain silent.

"Karliss is an adept student?" he asked. Jaygin dared not ask what his son was best at.

"Quite, but you knew that in Frilan's Notch. Puaul says languages are his strongest hand, though he excels at nearly everything he sets his mind to."

Jaygin swallowed a sigh of relief at that. "I am glad to hear it."

They stopped at the archway into the library, Jaygin's heart skipping merrily at the sound of his son's voice in a long-dead language.

"He speaks Seh nearly as well as if he was born to it," Elb imparted.

"He was, and you know it. You spoke the words yourself." His voice was rough. The memories of that night still haunted him.

"What do you seek, Jaygin?" Elb whispered.

Jaygin shook his head. He wasn't certain what he sought, past reassurances that Karliss was still the son he'd raised and loved. Would the priests steal him not with laws and motions but with permission where Jaygin had offered resistance? The thought of it had tortured him, day and night, until he'd decided to visit.

"Come. Karliss will be happy to see you."

He doubted it, but he took the step forward that would place him within view of anyone at the closest tables.

Master Puaul's animated discussion with Karliss broke off, and he raised his dark head from the book set between them. He didn't offer greeting, seemingly questioning Jaygin's arrival silently.

Jaygin stared at Karliss. His bare chest was deeply tanned, and he'd started growing masculine curls on it. The table covering hid the rest of him, leaving Jaygin to wonder at what he'd chosen to wear. There was little doubt that Elb would bow to whatever choice Karliss made for himself.

It took a moment for Karliss to react to the break in his lesson. He raised his gaze to Master Puaul, then followed his line of sight to the doorway. His eyes widened, and his smile broke free. In a heartbeat,

Karliss was on his feet, rounding the table at a run to grasp Jaygin around the chest.

"I missed you. Are Mother and Kev with you?"

"Not this time," Jaygin managed to say. He thanked Magmon silently that Karliss was still the honest, expressive boy who'd left Frilan's Notch. True, his son now wore the waist wrap that Elb wore, but he was largely of the same temperament.

Karliss pulled back, his face glowing in happiness. "Will you be staying long?"

"A few days. Spring holidays are too far."

His son sighed. "I agree. I wish Kev had come, but I suppose he's busy with his own schooling."

"Indeed."

Elb cut into the conversation smoothly. "We could put off Lord Karliss's lessons for the duration of your—"

"No," Jaygin decreed. "I have interrupted his lessons in my haste to see him. Attend to Master Puaul." He offered a tip of his head to the cleric. "We will meet again for dinner?"

Karliss affected a deep sigh. "You *could* have agreed. But, yes. I would enjoy that very much."

Jaygin laughed heartily at that. "I am sure you would rather have me permit you a third holiday this year, but I—"

"Value my education too much to—"

He turned his son and nudged him toward the table. "Go on. Go on. Complain to me at dinner. Your lessons await."

Karliss looked back, casting him an impish grin that said he would try to gain that holiday yet.

Elb's hand closed on Jaygin's shoulder, though he addressed them both. "You may use my private dining chamber. I will join the other masters for the meal."

* * * *

Jaygin made the final turn toward the rooftop, then stopped to catch his breath. Karliss was certain to remain in top form with such a climb twice daily.

It was nearly an hour until dinner bell, but since he'd learned his son's lessons ended two hours before it, he couldn't contain himself any longer. On that thought, he jogged up the remaining stairs, giving thanks for the gauze tunics Elb had ordered delivered to his rooms.

Karliss's rooms were empty, and a waist wrap was tossed over the prayer bench. Jaygin winced at the probable truth. Karliss loved to swim, and he'd often sought out the communal baths and rooftop pond in his second—very naked—year.

He took a calming breath and headed for the pond. Outside, he considered only a moment before he chose the stone path to the back of the pond. It was longer and less scenic, but it would preserve his dinner clothes.

Jaygin stopped short inside the stand of high leafy plants that shaded the pond. He stared at Karliss, his stomach clenching.

The woman in his son's arms was face-to-face with him in the belly-deep water. Their mouths were meshed in an involved and carnal kiss. She was dark enough of skin to be a native, but nearly assured to be of Aidalyn or Volcalen birth by her deep red hair.

It took a moment for Jaygin to fully internalize that it wasn't simply a kiss they were engaged in. Her knees lightly breached the rippling water and disappeared again. His son's tightening and loosening muscles announced the fact that Karliss was guiding the woman up and down his cock.

She broke off the kiss, crying out softly, her head thrown back in pleasure. "Slowly," she breathed. "Exist in the moment."

Karliss chuckled. "You lie to yourself. Slow is not what you want."

A smile curved her kiss-plumped lips up. "Well done, Kar. Show me what I want."

There was no mistaking what followed. Karliss was merciless in his sexual mastery of her, far too knowing to be new to the art. His thrusts were smooth and sure.

In moments, her moans became screams of climax and his groans and grunts a roar of the same. Karliss brought his mouth down on hers again, ravenous as Jaygin was when Karliss had been conceived.

Jaygin noted miserably that he was hard himself, aroused by the combination of memories of his days of being filled with Magmon's fire and watching his son thus afflicted.

The woman broke off the kiss, smiling sweetly. "Not today, Kar," she counseled.

Karliss grumbled a curse, seemingly furious with her for her refusal. Her hand cupped his face, and his muscles eased, the hunger in his expression renewed.

"You have a dinner to prepare for," she crooned.

Karliss stared at her and then shook off her hand. He eased her down his body. "Yes, I do." His voice was even, without emotion to speak of which he'd rather do, given the choice. Karliss didn't speak to her again...not to ask for her return nor to apologize for his brevity.

The woman watched him swim the length of the pond. He climbed out the marble staircase and bolted down the dirt path, taking the shortest way back to his rooms.

Jaygin grimaced at the fact that Karliss was still erect...and the fact that he was, as well.

Karliss's lover turned with a smile, wading to the stone path. The waist wrap she donned was in Magmon's red, marking her as a priestess concubine of the higher orders. She ambled up the path, seemingly lost in memories of his son...until she spied Jaygin.

Her smile faded, and her eyes went wide. She glanced toward the pond, then back to Jaygin. "Mi'lord," she offered shakily.

"Priestess," he grumbled in return. Jaygin saved her the awkward moment by turning away and hurrying to the stairs.

He didn't slow until he'd let the drape swing shut behind him in Elb's dining chamber. As he expected, the high priest had a bottle of hard spirits set on the sidebar. Jaygin poured himself a tumbler, gulping it down. He squeezed his weeping eyes shut, gasping at the burn searing his throat.

Magmon's fire! Will I never escape it? Will Karliss?

That was a useless question. His son had been touched by Magmon, conceived in the god's fire, born in it, and consumed by it daily. Jaygin couldn't imagine enduring the burn for an extended period of time.

The spirits beckoned, and Jaygin poured himself another tumbler. That time, he sipped at it.

The drape moved. Jaygin didn't turn to it. Karliss wouldn't have cleaned and dressed that quickly, which meant the interloper was Elb.

"What do you want of me, Elb?" he asked wearily. *Anything but my son. I was promised they wouldn't ask that of me.*

"What is it *you* want? Why are you here?"

There were no words for that but the truth. "I do not want him to change. Karliss is still a child."

"When you saw him in the library, was he not the son who left you in Frilan's Notch?"

Jaygin took another sip of the liquid fire. "He was, but at the pond he—"

"He hurried from Sulin the moment he realized the time."

No doubt, the young priestess had reported the entire scene to Elb.

The high priest continued.

"Your son cannot abide the wait to see you, as you could not abide the—"

"He is too young to play such games!"

Elb sighed. "Karliss does not play the love games young lords do. You are right; he is too young to understand them. When he reaches twenty, he will have no need or want of them."

Jaygin turned to him, his confusion deepened by the alcohol rush into his bloodstream. "Then what do you call his amusements?"

"You have felt Magmon's fire, Jaygin. You confessed to me once that you had considered and dismissed what your son was, based on when and how he was conceived."

"I felt the god's fire with my *wife*."

"And you had no control of it. You admitted as much. For two days, you could think of nothing else."

"I was an adult. Thirty-two when Karliss was conceived. Twice his age."

"And still shockingly young to be settled with a wife and planting your seed. As I recall, your father was—"

"And what of that?" Jaygin challenged. "Will we have bastard heirs to the Furian throne from within your temple?" Since the male contraceptive herbals were not for use by sub-adults, he wasn't certain whether to hope they weren't chancing pregnancy or that they were.

"You will not," Elb stated calmly.

"And am I to trust this?"

"The He-Atal feel the burn, but they do not reproduce until Magmon descends fully again."

Jaygin staggered to a chair and sank into it. Somehow, the tumbler of spirits made it there without spilling. "When Magmon..." He took a calming breath. "You mean, when he meets the Ician."

"Her name is Diama. She has just taken her place as Ician."

There was no way to tackle that subject. He'd thought it was insane that the He-Atal weren't told their destinies before he knew the current incarnation was to be his own son. Now that it was, he felt more secure in that determination.

Jaygin turned his mind back to other subjects, at a loss to balk tradition on the meeting to come. "I still do not care for this. Karliss moves like a man who has played the games for years instead of less than a season."

"And he spoke not a word of Seh when he arrived here, Jaygin."

"What has that to do with—"

"You remember the burn of Magmon's fire," Elb stated.

Jaygin felt his cheeks heat. "It is not the sort of thing one forgets."

"You felt it for two days."

"I am well aware of how long I—"

"Karliss feels Magmon's fire every day of his life and has for the last year. Still, he attends to more than the burn. Can you say the same of the time you felt it?"

"You know I cannot," he grumbled. Jaygin and Elia hadn't paused long enough to eat a full meal, in his fervor.

"Your son is strong, Jaygin, and yet..." Elb paused, closing his eyes as if pained.

"And yet?" he repeated.

"You remember his first two years. You remember how Karliss fought daily to control the fire in his blood?"

"You know I do." His heart ached at the memories of Elia's tears, of her screaming in the middle of the night. "Every time he chilled in a heated room or went limp in fever, I felt helpless as a kitten."

"He fights that fight again, Jaygin. Karliss has so little control, I dare not trust him with anyone but priestess concubines."

Jaygin couldn't be certain if the vertigo that washed over him came from the truth of his son's condition or the onset of a horrific drunk. The one sure thing was that he would not tell Elia this and worry her with it.

Worse, the god's fire might burn for years, as it had the first time. How would they handle it? If Karliss was forbidden to return to Frilan's Notch, Elia would glean the reason why. "And when he comes home? Or will you refuse him that?"

Elb settled next to him, taking the tumbler from his hand and drinking it down. "He seldom fevers. Not since his first days in the temple."

There was a moment of tense expectation.

"But his hungers are strong. When he returns home, Karliss will come to the temple at Frilan's Notch for...instruction. His mother need never know why, and you need not fear his control."

"Priestesses?" Jaygin guessed.

"Have you a better plan?"

"No," he admitted. "None."

CHAPTER SIX

Karliss jogged along the corridor, his heart speeding in excitement.

He berated himself as the first stroke of the dinner bell tolled. He was late to see his own father, because he'd been too busy enjoying the gifts of a priestess. Karliss grimaced at the stark truth of it.

Magmon sear it! When Sulin reminded him that dinner was approaching, Karliss had been mortified. Was Magmon's fire more important to him than his father was?

"Never," he vowed.

He launched through the drape into Master Elb's dining chamber, stopping in surprise at the sight of the high priest lounging with his father. "My apologies," he offered. He searched his memories and their expressions for some sign that he was facing punishment, but neither bore that out.

"For?" Jaygin inquired, his smile widening. "The bell still tolls. You are not late yet, Karliss."

Master Elb sipped at an alcoholic drink, nodding his head. "If you gentlemen will excuse me..." He rose to leave.

"We will speak again soon, Elb," his father promised.

Karliss worked at that. His father called the high priest by name, with no titles? How had such a thing happened? Prince or not, the clergy had titles that even his king-grandfather would be expected to use.

"That we will, Jaygin."

As would the clergy be expected to use a royal or nobleman's title. Before he could open his mouth to question this strange situation, the high priest clapped a hand on his father's shoulder and then Karliss's, shocking him to silence again. He disappeared through the drape, leaving Karliss alone with his father for the first time in months.

The calm was short-lived. Any attempt either of them wanted to make to strike up conversation was preempted by the rush of priestesses through the drape. They brought plates of food, drinks, and bowls of fruit.

Once their bounty of refreshment was arranged on the table, they bowed to Karliss and left without a word.

Karliss shifted nervously, glancing at Jaygin out of the corner of his eyes. "They... They should not do that," he managed to stammer out.

His father laughed heartily. "You are a Furian prince, Karliss. People will certainly bow to you."

"As are you. Bowing to me and not to you—"

"It is nothing to concern yourself about. They are accustomed to your presence. I am new to the temple."

Karliss hesitated.

"Sit. Let us eat," Jaygin invited, waving a hand to the empty chair opposite his position.

He settled in the chair, abruptly self-conscious. Jaygin started to eat, and Karliss did the same, but it wasn't like the comfortable meals they'd passed at home. He couldn't fathom the difference, but there was one. What could have changed so much in the few months he'd been in Magmalen? Would his friends studying in Volcalen find their first dinners with their fathers as uncomfortable?

His father stared at him, seemingly searching for something Karliss couldn't name.

"Is there a problem, Father?"

"You have grown so much in two short months." His voice was wistful. "You left a boy, but you are becoming a man in my absence."

"Surely not a man," he protested weakly. At times, Karliss felt like a boy, moments like now. At others, as when the priestesses gifted him, he felt like a man. Karliss wasn't certain what he was.

Jaygin was silent for a moment. "Do you like life at the temple?"

He considered that. "I do, but I miss you all."

"Here or at Volcalen, it was time for you to leave us."

Karliss nodded, his mood grim. "I suppose that is true."

"As long as you are happy here."

"I am. My rooms... I cannot imagine I would see something half as grand at Volcalen, prince or not. You should come see them, Father."

"I *have* seen them, and you are correct. Volcalen has nothing to compare with the beauty of the temple at Magmalen."

Karliss lowered his fork, repeating his father's words in his mind. "You have seen them? When would you have seen them?" Surely not while Karliss attended to his lessons. It went against the rules of the temple.

Jaygin's brow furrowed. "When would I..." His eyes widened. "They did not tell you? I thought you knew."

His heart pounded hard against his ribs, and his stomach clenched. There were many things Karliss wasn't told. There were countless things he'd asked only to be offered platitudes, half-answers, and refusals of answers. "Tell me what? What should they have told me, Father?"

"This is not the first time you have lived in the temple at Magmalen, Karliss. You... We *all* passed your first two years here."

"We did?" Karliss searched for memories of the temple, but none presented themselves. "I thought we'd always lived in Frilan's Notch. Or perhaps that I'd been born in Aidalyn, and we'd moved to Frilan's Notch after the last great flooding."

Jaygin smiled. "Not at all. Well, you *were* born in Aidalyn, but we lived here afterward."

"But...why?" And why had no one told him?

"For your health. We were told that the chill, wet weather in Aidalyn would kill you...then. I imagine you could tolerate it now."

"I was a sickly child?" he asked, horrified that so momentous a secret had been kept from him.

Jaygin laughed heartily, until a tear escaped his eye. "One would not believe it to see you run from room to room with the priests and priestesses in chase."

"But I was?"

He sobered. "No. I cannot believe you were in much danger, but a father does not chance his son."

Karliss took a bite of the roasted meat, abruptly uncertain.

"You were everywhere at once," his father mused, seemingly lost in happy memories. "In the communal baths, in the offices and sleeping areas... and, despite all the guards set to prevent it, in the pond and rooftop gardens."

"The pond? I love the pond." Was that the reason he loved it? Did some corner of his mind harbor images of frolicking as a babe?

"You have always loved it. Your mother requested the rooftop rooms, but the priests would hear none of it."

"Because they feared I would drown in the pond?" It seemed a farfetched concern, especially considering what an accomplished swimmer he was.

"Or fall off the roof, I imagine. You were energy in a shell of skin."

Karliss chewed a bite of sorba melon, then met his father's gaze. "Why am I here? Why not Volcalen? You said I could survive the weather now."

Jaygin's jaw tightened, and he stared at his plate. "I also said that a father does not risk his son."

"Then I *am* fragile."

"I do not believe that," his father grumbled.

"You *do* believe it, or I would be in Volcalen." Breathing was abruptly difficult. Was this how his body failed him? Was this what they feared? "Will I ever lead? Or will you refuse to chance me?" Furian kings always led from Aidalyn.

His father sighed deeply, pushing his food around the plate aimlessly. "You will lead, if it is the will of Magmon that you do."

Karliss's appetite fled. He rose, feeling ill. His training was likely very different than what he'd learn in Volcalen. He was learning Seh. Were any of his friends doing that? No one he knew but priests and priestesses spoke Seh. Was he being trained for something other than the throne?

"Karliss?" Jaygin looked up, his color dipping.

"I...I need air."

He pushed to his feet. "Karliss?"

Karliss motioned his father back to his chair with a shaking hand. "Tomorrow... Breakfast. I promise, but for now..."

"I will be here. Go, now."

Karliss fled into the corridor, running aimlessly, taking turns and stairs without plan or reason. He didn't want to return to his rooms. The gardens and pond suddenly seemed sinister. He didn't want to speak to Master Elb. But where else would he go?

"Lord Karliss?"

He turned toward the voice, stumbling over his feet. His efforts to right himself a loss, he slammed into the wall, back first. His head cracked hard against the stone, and Karliss winced, pressing a hand against it.

"Lord Karliss!"

A woman's body nestled to his, her hand searching out the lump beneath his.

"I should call for a priestess healer and—"

"No. I am not fragile," he insisted. Had he always been treated thus and never noted it?

Her breasts brushed against his chest, enflaming him, invigorating him. The last thing he felt was fragile.

"You are bleeding," she pleaded. "You—"

He pulled her face to his, urging her lips open for a kiss. She didn't protest it; her hand smoothed his hair down, encouraging him to continue.

Karliss pulled away, focusing blearily on Lurai. "Did you know I had lived here as a babe?" he asked.

She nodded solemnly.

"Do you think I am fragile?"

"No. Never."

He believed her. "Come to my bed. I...need you to agree, just this once, Lurai."

She deliberated only a moment, then nodded.

They passed precious few people on the way. None of them attempted to stop them; none questioned them. All backed away with bowed heads and murmured acknowledgements.

Karliss didn't waste a moment. The door closed behind them, a door he'd never bothered with before. He pulled Lurai into his arms.

As if sensing his urgency, she opened the fasteners on his wrap. He pushed hers up her thighs. They crossed the room, wrapped in each other's arms, falling to the bed together.

Then he was buried inside her, driving them both over in moments. It was not enough; Karliss needed more. It wasn't a night for a priestess to call a halt.

* * * *

"What in Magmon's fire did you say to him?" Elb thundered.

Jaygin groaned, his head and stomach swirling opposite directions. "You are not permitted to enter my rooms without asking my—"

"When Karliss is at stake, I go where I must. What did you say?"

Something in that comment cut through the fuzz in his head. "At stake? What has happened?"

"That is what I am asking you, *Lord* Jaygin."

"We spoke about his early days in Magmalen."

"Why would you?"

Jaygin rubbed hands to his throbbing head. "What the blazes did you let me drink?"

"Frial Ice Breath. A decade old. Now, what was said?"

His stomach gave a warning lurch, and a cold sweat broke out on his body. "Never again. I swear it to Magmon, the Dragon God." In his state, it couldn't hurt to use the Fire God's formal title.

"Answer me straight, or you will swear it personally, in the god's lair."

"I am not certain I am not now."

"Answers, Jaygin!"

He groaned, swallowing down the urge to vomit. "Karliss believes I see him as physically fragile, weak...sickly."

"Are you mad? Why would you tell him such a thing?"

"I did not tell him that. I... *You* forbade me to tell him his destiny."

"It is against tradition. You know that," Elb snapped at him.

"The only reason I had left to give him for his presence here was the fact that Aidalyn would have killed him as a babe."

The stillness of the room was so complete and abrupt it unnerved Jaygin, and he opened his eyes, searching out Elb.

The high priest stood over him, pale and tense. "You are correct about that. I never thought to explain it. Karliss is an adept young student. His mind questions always."

"What has happened to my son?"

"He took a priestess to his bed."

"Is that all? But...I thought—"

"They are ordered not to stay the night. If Lurai did so, she must have felt it an emergency."

"What sort of emergency?"

Elb sighed. "I know only that those who saw them together said Karliss burned in Magmon's fury...and Lurai had blood on her hand. I waited all night, hoping the young priestess would leave him to report to me, but that hasn't happened."

Jaygin started to question him, his mind working hard at Elb's claim that Karliss lacked control. If he hurt the girl—

Elb spoke over him. "There were no sounds of distress. I am certain it's not that."

He forced himself to sitting, grinding his teeth against a wave of nausea. "And you have done nothing but wait and listen for the girl to scream for aid?" What madness was this?

"With no knowledge of what sent him over the edge of reason? Certainly not!"

Jaygin reached for his trousers. "I will go to him."

"Perhaps—"

"He is my son, Elb."

The high priest hesitated, then nodded his agreement.

* * * *

"Karliss."

He yawned, burying his cheek in the pillow. It was too early to rise for lessons. The first breakfast bell, the one for young training priests, hadn't tolled yet.

"Karliss."

He grumbled a complaint, wishing his father away.

A feminine gasp pierced the fog of his mind. He opened his eyes to the sight of Lurai's open-mouthed look of surprise.

"Karliss? Ah, good. You are awake."

The words to reply stuck in his throat. He nodded, then groaned, pressing his fingertips to the lump at the back of his skull.

"I know how you feel," Jaygin imparted, sounding more than a little weary.

"You struck your head as well?" Karliss didn't seek out his father's expression. Instead, he motioned Lurai to go.

She smoothed her wrap under the cover of the quilts.

"No. I drank too much of Elb's Ician...whatever the blazes it is called."

Lurai rose from the bed, smoothing the cover over Karliss without looking back. She hurried away with a muttered word of greeting for Jaygin.

"You didn't get her wrap off?" his father chided. "It is better skin-to-skin, you know."

"I know. I have had her wrap off bef—" Karliss choked in the realization of what he was saying and to whom.

Jaygin's laughter rang out, making Karliss's head ache. In the state his father was in, it probably made his head ache as well, but still he laughed.

"Is she a favorite? This Lurai?"

"The priestesses discourage showing favoritism." *Save that first time. Alina had nearly demanded he do so then.* "But I do favor the lighter northern ones," he admitted.

"I suppose that makes a certain amount of sense," he answered cryptically.

Karliss shot him a look of warning, noting his father's smile fading in satisfaction. "I am growing very weary of that."

The last of the smile disappeared into an expression of confusion. "Of what?"

"Half answers. Non-answers. Cryptic replies. Why am I denied knowledge of myself? How can I ever know what sort of man I will be, if there are lies and unspoken secrets about my youth?"

"Was there ever a worse morning to be questioned thus?"

"At least you get answers."

Jaygin sighed. "I can only answer what I know, Karliss."

"You will?" His heart skipped in excitement.

"I will."

Karliss took a calming breath, ordering his aching mind. "What made you believe I was so frail that I required the southern reaches?"

He took his time, pulling a chair up and sinking into it, his gaze far away. Jaygin seemed to age a decade in moments, as if the memories were something odious to him, something he'd tried to forget. He squeezed his eyes shut and then opened them again. "You were blue with cold, even wrapped in quilts. You burned in fevers. I have never been more frightened in my life."

Karliss nodded, his stomach clenching at the thought of it. "I was very sick, then."

"Truthfully?" He paused for a moment long enough to set Karliss's heart pounding. "No. You were a hearty child. But I was young, Karliss. I had no idea what other course to take. The priests suggested this, for your safety, and I vowed to follow through.

"You were so much better here. The fevers were infrequent, and you had a chance to grow strong. I would have agreed to anything that would keep you safe from harm. Except the loss of you. No one asked it, of course, but that was the one line I'd drawn myself."

"And what did they ask? What did they suggest...and you agree to?"

He hesitated. "Only training you here instead of in Volcalen. I agreed not to chance you, even now, when you haven't been ill for so many years. I swear it."

Karliss breathed a sigh of relief. "Did you know? About the priestess concubines? Did you know I was..." He wasn't certain what the polite way to broach the subject was.

"Not until last night, but I suspected it."

Karliss felt it difficult to meet his father's gaze steadily. "You did not state your feelings on the matter."

"Because they are of no consequence."

"Are they not? You taught me—"

"Your mother and I taught you the ways to act in polite society," his father interjected. "The temple, center of learning in the southern reaches though it may be, is not polite society." He seemed amused by that.

"Then...you approve?" He chanced a look at Jaygin.

"The priests and priestesses of Magmon have counseled us well all your life, Karliss. They have never brought you harm."

"And?" he prompted. The need for his father's approval beat at him as it rarely had before.

"You will meet your priestesses at the temple in Frilan's Notch. I...understand your needs, though your mother will not approve. It is better that you enjoy the company of priestesses than play your hand at the games of the nobles. We will tell your mother that you have lessons to attend to at the temple."

Karliss resisted the urge to ask again.

"I approve, Karliss."

He sighed in relief.

Jaygin seemed to struggle with something of great importance. "You should not feel the need to hide from me. I am your father." He hesitated. "The honest expression of passion is nothing to hide."

That sounded like something Master Elb would say. "I never realized you were so religious."

He looked to the roof over their heads, a tight smile pulling up at the corners of his lips. "Aside from my prayers on the night of your birth, I never realized I was, either. And, perhaps, those on the night of your conception."

Karliss laughed.

"And now... I believe you offered me breakfast."

He laughed harder. "In *your* condition?" he teased.

"You see the priestess healers for your head, and I will see one for mine. After that, we will see to breakfast."

Karliss nodded.

"I may even see my way clear to excusing you from studies for a day or two." His father's smile was all too knowing.

CHAPTER SEVEN

Kar sipped at the glass of tura berry wine, trying not to laugh outright at the pathetic attempts the other young men were making at attracting the fairer sex.

Laysen returned to the bar, ordering an ale. "I notice you are not trying your hand, Kar," he challenged.

"At that?" He gave up the battle and laughed. "I haven't been that clumsy in three years."

His childhood friend scowled at him. "Liar," he accused.

"Nay, nay, my dear Laysen. While you have been slaving away in Volcalen, enduring lectures on propriety and civilized behavior, administered by dowager house matrons, I have been educated by the priestess concubines in Magmalen."

"Liar," he repeated, though a little less forcefully.

Kar lifted his glass in mock challenge. "I had my first two within an hour of reaching the temple...together."

Laysen choked on his ale, darkening. "You are mad, Karliss Furia."

Kar drained the last of his wine and set his glass down. "Very well, then. I am mad. For your education alone, I will leave the barroom with a woman within half an hour. A quarter, if I choose my partner well."

"Without paying her," Laysen qualified.

"You *pay* women?" Kar asked, stunned by the notion.

"No. Of course not, but I want to make certain you do not, either."

Kar laughed heartily at the thought. "I do not need to."

He looked around, evaluating the choices that presented themselves. Kar immediately disqualified the giggling girls looking to make an advantageous marriage. Being a prince was enough to sway them. It would take no skill and not present the challenge he'd agreed to.

He dismissed those who were desperate or drunk. That was as deplorable as paying a woman to bed her.

That left him with two women at the far end of the bar. They were older, unmarried. *Or, perhaps from unhappy marriages or widowed.* By their expressions, he could gauge they knew their wants and were bored with the young men trying their hands at seduction. *Perfect.*

Kar pushed to his feet and smoothed his collar.

"No, Kar," Laysen whispered. "You do not want to try to sway Lady Amil and her sister."

"If they refuse me, there are others." But none he wanted as much and none that would offer a challenge to his skills.

"I will put flowers on your grave," his friend quipped.

"I thank you for your kindness."

Kar strode across the barroom, meeting Lady Amil's gaze solidly. She stared at him, as if in disbelief that Kar dared approach her.

He scooped her hand up as if they were old friends, brushing his lips across her knuckles. "Lady Amil," he greeted her, stroking his fingertips in slow circles over the pulse point in her wrist.

"Lord Karliss Furia?" she guessed, breathless already.

Other heads turned, but Kar ignored them, focusing on the Lady Amil. A woman liked to think you saw only her. She deserved that attention, when you were asking her to gift you her body. He bowed his head in confirmation of his name. "The same."

Her sister moved a step closer, shooting a look of confusion at him. She offered her hand. "Melia," she informed him.

Kar took hers without releasing the first, extending the same treatment to Melia he had to her sister. For a moment, neither of them spoke.

Lady Amil forced out a shaky question. "Is it true you study at the temple in Magmalen?"

"Diligently." Kar put a wealth of meaning into that word.

Melia glanced at their joined hands, then shot a sideward glance at her sister. "Which of us do you desire, mi'lord?"

That being a question with the highest possibility of alienating them, he didn't hesitate to offer the single answer sure to entice them. "Both."

"You jest." But Melia's hand remained in his, as did her sister's.

He smiled, raising both of their wrists to kiss at the pulse points. "A man never jests with beautiful women."

Lady Amil smiled sweetly. "You are certain of yourself," she noted. Her tone said she wasn't nearly as certain.

"I am, but with good reason."

"I suspect you intend one of us for Lord Laysen," she continued.

"I *intend*, with your agreement, to bring both of you to bliss with my mouth and hands...then with my cock. No one but myself."

Melia made a sound of longing, half-swallowed. Kar pretended not to notice, though his heart raced in excitement.

Lady Amil wrapped her hand around his. "And if you fail?" she asked.

"I never fail, but if I do... I am certain the entire city will know of it."

"You accept that?"

"Since I never fail, why would I balk at it? Surely, such a cultured lady as yourself wouldn't lie about such a thing."

The sisters stared at each other. Melia tipped her head toward Kar in an unspoken and unknown communication.

"Perhaps a kiss to prove my...oral prowess?" he suggested.

"Wise, do you think?" Melia asked.

"Satisfactory," Lady Amil agreed.

"Very well." Kar leaned toward her, releasing both hands and planting one of his on the bar behind her.

Lady Amil met him open-mouthed, probably trying to embarrass or unnerve Kar. He met her avidly, widening her lips and sweeping inside. She was bored with uneducated boys, but Kar hadn't been that in four years, and Magmalen had taught him ease with his sexuality, even with an audience.

He parted from her slowly, noting Lady Amil's harsh breathing in satisfaction. "Now, your dear sister, mi'lady."

Melia sank back to the bar at his approach, seemingly seeking support for her lightly trembling form. Kar leaned to the right, releasing the bar with his left hand and planting the other beside the younger sister.

For all her bravado, Melia was less comfortable with their public display. Kar made that kiss a slow, patient affair, a taste of what he intended for them and not the carnal vow he'd made to Lady Amil.

Kar eased away again, watching Melia's eyes slide open. "Have I interested you?" he asked.

"Yes," Melia breathed.

Lady Amil was silent for a long moment. "I would say so, Lord Karliss."

"Kar, mi'lady." He'd come to love the nickname the priestess concubines had given him.

Her dark eyes crinkled at the corners. "Since we will be so intimate, you should call me Missa."

"I shall." Kar turned and offered his arms. "Shall we, ladies?"

Melia was at his left arm in the blink of an eye, winding her arm through his. Missa took his right a moment later. Across the room, he saw Laysen look up from his conversation with Nabin and Rennel, wide-mouthed.

Kar ignored them, looking from one of his companions to the other. "You will never regret this show of trust," he vowed.

"I trust not," Melia replied.

They ambled to the door, passing Laysen without comment. Out of the corner of his eye, he saw Rennel pluck the money from Laysen's hand. He bit back a laugh. They were betting on Kar's sexual prowess. He'd never heard of something so ridiculous.

Melia's home was only two streets away, and it couldn't come fast enough for Kar.

The door closed behind them, and Missa dismissed her steward.

Melia paused for a moment, seemingly uncertain.

Kar took the opportunity to wrap his arms around her. "The lounge, the bed, or the bath?" he asked.

She sucked in a startled breath.

He continued, trying to put her at ease with what he intended for them. "I would suggest the bed or bath. A lounge is so cramped that—"

"The bed," she decided.

Missa pressed to his back. "A bed does sound enticing."

Kar drew Melia to his chest, his cock hardening in anticipation. "Yes, it most certainly does. Lead the way?"

Melia nodded and turned, rushing down the corridor toward the private chambers.

Missa tarried behind, stroking at Kar's length as if in contemplation. She sighed. "An early riser never lasts."

"No man lasts as I do, Missa."

"We shall see." She rounded him, putting an extra sway in her step to entice him.

As if I need enticing? Kar followed, turning into the bedroom a moment after Missa did.

It was a woman's space, silks and lace ruffles in cream and rose. The bed itself was as large as his bed in Magmalen, which meant it was large enough for three with ease.

Melia stood beside the bed, her arms stretched behind her in an effort to undo the fasteners a maid normally would. Kar stepped to her back, taking over. He buried his mouth against her neck, drinking in her scent as he made it rise for him.

Her muscles eased, and she tipped her head to one side, moaning. Melia reached one hand back, wrapping it in Kar's hair. The dress dipped, held to her body by the arm hooked around him and nothing else.

Kar guided the arm down, pushing the dress off her wrist. It slipped down her body and pooled at her ankles.

"You are very good," Missa noted. "No man has put my sister at ease so quickly."

He turned Melia and eased her to the mattress, meeting Missa's gaze as he spread her sister's legs.

Missa nodded, sliding her dress off her shoulder. "Melia will be short duty for you. I will not."

"I will savor every moment with you both."

With that, Kar gave his full attention to Melia, noting her stunned expression. Missa was correct. It would take very little to send her over.

Still, he gave her his best. Kar used his hands and mouth to tease her body to a potent edge and then plunge her over. When Melia lay in the aftermath of her climax, he turned to Missa.

The older sister lay full out on the bed, watching them. Her fingers stroked idly at her clit, not enough to send her over but enough to coat them in a slick of her ready body. "You know your way around a woman's body, Kar."

"I do." He stalked over the bed toward her.

"Your clothing off, if you please," she requested. "Silk is a delight, but I prefer a man's skin against mine."

"Skin-to-skin is better," he agreed. Kar stripped off his silk tunic, then his low boots, socks, and trousers.

Missa licked her lips, taking in all of him. "Luscious," she complimented him.

Kar laid out over her, fitting his hips to hers. "I could return that compliment a dozen times over, Missa."

She pulled his head down, kissing him much as she had at the bar. The lady was starved for a man who knew his way around a bedroom. Still, he knew she wanted the encounter to last.

He eased down her body, trailing lips and hands over her heated flesh. "You will be the first to feel my length, Missa," he vowed. "Then Melia."

She nodded, writhing against his tongue on her shaven mound.

"Would you like me between you? Arousing you again?" Kar sucked her nub into his mouth, batting at it slowly with his tongue.

"Yes." Her voice was a ragged gasp.

He'd known she would when she watched him with Melia. "Promise me a boon," he bargained. Kar guessed it was one they would like.

"What boon?"

"When both of you have tasted my full length..." He nibbled at her seam and then buried his tongue inside her.

"Yes!"

Melia was moving again, her hands stroking up his back.

Missa was at the edges of reason already. It was time to prove his prowess. He ate at her ravenously, groaning as she shattered around him and poured her musk into his mouth.

His aching cock didn't have long to suffer the wait. Kar was asking a boon, and he'd earn it.

He rose up over her, his chin coated in a slick of Missa's fluids. She screamed in delight as he slid his cock into her still-spasming body.

Kar kissed her, using her flavor to drive Missa from one release to another. He reared back, wrapping one hand around Melia's neck to draw her into his kiss, balancing his pistoning body on her sister.

Missa's orgasms ran together, at least three before he poured into her in climax. That didn't mean he went flaccid. Melia's fervor kept him hard and hungry for more.

When Missa collapsed to the mattress, panting in the overload of sexual stimuli, Kar slid from her body and rolled away, pulling Melia over him. He was inside her in an instant, hissing out a curse at how tight she was. Melia's screams put her elder sister's to shame, and she rode him hard, meeting Kar thrust for thrust.

Missa appeared at his side, her mouth seeking out his. It was nearly what he wanted, so close it made him crazed.

She nipped at his woman-flavored chin. "What boon did you want?" she purred.

Kar traced her lower lip, smiling at how kiss-plumped it was. "Your mouth...while I take Melia into my mouth again."

Her eyes dilated, and she hummed out a note of interest. "And then?"

"I promised to lie between you and arouse you again. Only Magmon knows where we will end this night."

Melia climaxed again, her body milking him, her screams echoing off the walls. Kar followed her, certain Missa meant to agree to the boon.

He guided the half-conscious Melia up his body, positioning her sweet slit over his mouth. At the first touch of his tongue, her thighs shook, and she gasped out a plea for mercy.

Kar wouldn't have granted it for any reason. Melia was enjoying what he was doing, and this would be a most memorable night for her.

Missa's mouth engulfed him, and Kar knew he'd last longer than both of them combined.

* * * *

Kar ambled into the barroom, the top two buttons on his silk shirt undone and pleasantly exhausted.

Laysen looked up from the table he shared with Rennel and Nabin. "You did not," he grumbled.

Kar smiled, settling into an empty chair. "A most delightful pair." He yawned widely.

"You actually tumbled them both?" Nabin asked.

He nodded, hooked his hands behind his head, and stretched his back.

"How?" Laysen demanded. "How do you handle *two* women?"

"With a great amount of care and more than a little energetic activity."

Rennel leaned toward him, folding his arms on the tabletop. "*How* energetic?"

Kar laughed. "Very."

"How many times did you..." Laysen paused, seemingly at a loss. "You really *have* experienced two women at once before." He sounded hurt by the idea of it.

"I told you I had. Why would you doubt my word?" They never had before. *Of course, we've never discussed sexual exploits before.* Kar considered that, then rejected it, at a loss for what difference it could possibly make.

Laysen scowled. "Because most men our age would be lying about it."

Nabin snorted. "Most men my father's age would be lying."

Rennel nodded his agreement. "My grandfather's age, and he did not marry until he was nearly fifty and takes women still."

Kar shrugged, abruptly self-conscious.

"How many times did you?" Laysen repeated.

His face heated as it hadn't since his first months at the temple in Magmalen. "Did I? Did they? That is not the easiest question to answer, Laysen."

"You," Rennel suggested.

"They," Nabin countered.

"All of you," Laysen spoke over him.

Kar considered that. He pointed to Rennel. "Four."

Laysen choked.

He shifted his finger from Rennel to Nabin. "Women are harder to quantify. What may be several orgasms may also be one, drawn out."

"Guess," Nabin urged him.

"Assuming the close ones were one and not separate..." *I know some of them are separate. Why am I lying about it?* Kar pushed that thought away, feigning a recounting of the evening he didn't need to indulge in. "Five for Melia and four for Missa." In truth, he knew it was more than double that number.

He tipped his head to Laysen. "For a total of thirteen."

There was silence around the table.

Kar looked from one face to another, trying to find logic in their discomfort. *Or in mine.* "What is it?" he finally asked.

Laysen sighed. "There will be no women interested in us with you about." It sounded of an accusation.

Kar stood, trying not to wear his hurt as a mask. "I leave in ten days, and I imagine my father will be keeping me busy with affairs of state for the rest of my stay. I will not be in your way."

He strode away, ignoring the voices calling him back, confused for the first time in more than three years.

CHAPTER EIGHT

Jaygin looked up from the book he'd been enjoying, his smile at the sight of Elb fading. The high priest was tense, and that was always a bad omen.

"What is it, Elb?"

"Karliss..." He hesitated and glanced at the open doorway.

"I gathered that." What else would affect Elb this way?

The high priest looked toward the doors again, crossed the study, and shut them. He paused, seemingly collecting his thoughts.

"Elb?" he pressed him. "What is wrong?"

"Has Karliss been going to the bars with his friends in the evenings?"

"You know he has not. He did the first night home, but since then... Not at all."

Elb turned to him. "No. I did not know it. I suspected it."

Jaygin shook his head. "This concerns you, I see." If it didn't, Elb wouldn't be here, prodding for information.

"Why does he stay here? Does Karliss say?"

"He claims to have studies that keep him—"

Elb shook his head. "He has no studies. Not on his holiday." He seemed lost in thought.

"Must I drag this from you?" Jaygin fumed. "What is your concern?"

"Karliss has not sought out the priestesses, either. It has been nearly a week, Jaygin."

"I take it that concerns you?" A week of no sex was hardly newsworthy.

The high priest darkened. "Do you wish to know your son this well?" There was a hint of warning in the asking.

"You know I do, especially if something is wrong."

"Very well." He took a seat, arranging his robes for comfort. "Karliss has not gone more than three days without seeking a woman in four years. He rarely goes a day."

Jaygin ground his teeth. "Perhaps he is simply maturing," he suggested. He knew Elb would disagree with that sentiment, but it couldn't hurt to suggest it.

The high priest scowled at him. "This is no time for levity, Jaygin. Maturing would mean growing into Magmon's hunger, not losing touch with it."

"You said the priestesses were teaching him to control—"

Elb's look was enough to still his tongue.

"Very well. That is not the case. Do you suppose Karliss had a negative experience of some sort?" Jaygin knew the priests and priestesses had done their best to avoid it.

Elb went crimson. "As rumor has it, his experience was a positive one."

He rolled his eyes at the high priest's circumspect manner, considering what they were discussing. "And what does *rumor* say, Elb?"

"If you must know—"

"I believe I must," he replied acidly. If Elb wished Jaygin's help, the least the cleric could do was give him a full disclosure of the pertinent information.

"Lady Missa Amil and her sister Lady Melia Mia haunt the barrooms, hoping your son will make another appearance. It seems that Karliss—"

"I picture it well enough."

"Then you will understand my confusion. What could turn him away from youthful pursuits, especially when Magmon's fire sears him?"

Jaygin rose, setting the book next to the reading lamp lit for him. "I suppose I should find out the answer to that question."

"If you would." Elb rarely came this close to begging his help. It spoke his concern more than mere words ever could.

"You know I will," he grumbled, heading for Kar's rooms.

His elder son answered Jaygin's knock with a mumbled "enter," and he strolled inside.

Kar sat on his bed, dressed in trousers and a silk tunic, his bare feet tucked beneath him and a heavy book open on his lap. He didn't look up. "Did Master Elb send you?" he asked.

"No. Elb interrogated me, and I chose to come."

"To interrogate me," he persisted.

"To find out what is troubling you," he countered.

Kar didn't offer the information as Jaygin had hoped he would.

Jaygin settled at the foot of the mattress with a sigh. "Why are you avoiding the night life of the city?"

His son shrugged. "It...does not interest me."

"Lady Amil and Lady Mia interested you."

His hand tightened on the edge of the book. "For a moment," he conceded.

"You could go to the temple as you always have."

Kar shook his head, his expression stony.

"Women no longer appeal?" Jaygin pressed.

He shrugged again.

"You do not want to see your friends?"

"No." It was stated too firmly, too definitively to be chance, a sure sign that the answer lay there.

"Why not?"

"We have nothing in common."

"What? You grew together. You were boys—"

"*They* still are boys. I have not been for many years." A wry smile twisted his lips. "You said it yourself. I became a man nearly upon my arrival in Magmalen. It is..." His brow furrowed, as if he was uncertain how to proceed. "It was simply not apparent to me until now. Now that they proclaim themselves men...and I do...openly."

"Is it wrong to be more mature than your peers?"

"It is...awkward. They resent me."

"They resent you?" That made no sense at all.

Kar peeked up at him as he'd often done when he didn't want to say something directly.

"Because the women prefer you?" Jaygin guessed.

"Yes, and because I know things they never will."

"Know?" Realization nearly choked him. "Sexual...adventures?"

"They hardly care to know Seh."

Jaygin laughed shortly. "I imagine not."

Kar didn't join him. His son stretched his legs out, looking weary.

"Why avoid women? You are avoiding them, are you not?"

For a moment, Jaygin was certain he wasn't going to answer.

Kar closed his eyes, laying his head back. "Is it right?"

"Is what right?"

"I do not understand people. Oh, I understand *women*, but...but I have so little in common with other men."

Jaygin worked at the problem. "The men you deal with daily, you have no difficulty with."

"The priests, you mean. When I rule, I will have to deal with nobles, not priests. Or will I never lead? You never answered that question, as I recall."

"Because I do not know the answer to it. I will not stop you from it, if that is what you meant to ask."

Kar opened his eyes, the muscles at the back of his jaw working as if he was fighting asking something more. "Will Magmon's priests stop me?"

"They do not possess the power to. They could try to sway you not to take the throne, but such a thing would have started many years ago. Have they hinted at it?"

"No. Nothing like that."

"Then it is not their aim. The choice to rule or not is yours, Karliss." Other He-Atal had chosen the places they were born to eventually. Others had abandoned them, though none had abandoned Furia. What Kar did was his destiny to decide...even to abandoning Furia for the Frial Ician at her adulthood, though he wouldn't know that choice existed until it was upon him.

"The choice is mine?" He seemed wary of it.

"It is."

"Then I should learn to deal with the nobles."

"May I suggest something?" Jaygin worked at the most diplomatic way to present it.

Kar's eyes widened. "Would you? I admit to a certain loss on the subject."

Jaygin picked his words carefully, constructing what he hoped would express it best. "You had no problems dealing with your peers, until their definition of themselves as men centered around sexual conquest in the games."

He nodded. "I would agree. Please, go on."

"Avoid the games. Do not avoid the men. Direct the topics of conversation to areas where you are equals. Do not comment where you see the breach between you."

Kar seemed unconvinced.

"A man learns to be discreet in his sexual play over time. You have learned that lesson well and early. In another decade, they will learn it."

He groaned. "A decade."

"Possibly less. I learned it at twenty-five."

"And in the meantime?" Kar asked.

"If the bars thrill you, go occasionally. If not, take your priestesses. Do you hunt the bars in Magmalen?"

"I have not, as yet. The priests do not, so I never considered the possibility. I could, I suppose. I am certain Master Elb would allow it, now that I am an adult."

"I am certain he would." Jaygin managed to keep the sarcastic bite from his words by a hand's width.

Kar stared at a point on the wall, lost in thought.

"Would you like to share Elb's coach to the temple?" he offered. "I am certain he would wait for you to prepare."

"No."

"Should he expect you later this eve?"

Kar took longer to answer, wincing before he forced the word out. "No."

"Why? Why do you avoid women?"

He shrugged, seemingly unable to put his reservations into words.

Jaygin rose.

"Off to report to Master Elb?" his son snapped.

"I have nothing to report. I still do not understand your reasons."

"I do not understand my reasons," he admitted.

"It is part of becoming a man, Karliss. Everyone experiences it."

He sighed.

* * * *

Another knock interrupted his reading, and Kar ground his teeth in frustration. "Come in, Master Elb," he called out.

The door opened, but it wasn't the high priest entering. Lurai was dressed as a noblewoman might, her red-gold hair pulled up in a loose knot that left tendrils around her face.

His cock stiffened, and the room felt like an oven. The urge to have her naked on his sheets was so intense it made him lightheaded.

To have her at all. She'd been reassigned to another temple in his second year in Magmalen. He'd found that the priestess concubines often rotated among the temples. Aside from her form of dress, she hadn't changed much since he'd seen her last. His preference for her hadn't changed in the least.

Still, he had to know. "Are you dressed for the games or for polite company?" he inquired.

"Have there ever been games between us, Kar?" She shut the door, giving him an enticing view of her back.

His eyes lingered on the row of hooks. He'd had Lurai beneath him and above him many times. He knew every fingerwidth of her body, but he'd never realized how hungry the sight of her fully clothed could make him. It was a challenge.

Lurai turned back to him, folding her hands demurely and seemingly waiting for his response.

"We have known our share of games, I think," he offered diplomatically. This was just one more. He didn't doubt that Master Elb had summoned Lurai to shake Kar from his confusion and apathy.

She glided toward him, her cheeks an enticing pink now that she'd lost her southern tan. "Not when you have need of me. There are never games then."

The night he'd injured himself flashed through his mind. "And if I said I need you now?" he hinted.

"Do you? Or is there upset over nothing?" There was no taunt in that. With Lurai, he'd always known honest concern.

Kar considered her question. He couldn't remember ever being so confused, even that long-ago night. He needed more than comfort. He needed knowns instead of unknowns, unchanging relationships to counter the upheaval in others. "I need you, Lurai. Would you—"

"If you need me, I will be whatever you wish tonight."

He rose, padding to Lurai on bare feet. Kar tangled his fingers in her hair, brushing his lips over hers slowly, savoring as the priestesses had always told him to savor women.

Savoring Lurai was essential. No doubt, when his current upset was a memory, she'd move on to a temple far from him. All the priestesses left him eventually.

No, they go where the priests send them. It was nothing personal, nothing to do with Kar.

Their kisses were slow and deep, meaningless promises offered and accepted as he guided her to the bed. She didn't move to undress him, leaving the decision to progress to Kar. He was in no rush. He hadn't known she was leaving the last time he bedded her. This time he knew, and he wouldn't waste the gift Master Elb had offered him.

They sank to the mattress, exploring each other as if for the first time. In some ways, it was the first time. Kar had never taken his time with her before, not like they were now.

The burn of his arousal ignited into a bonfire of need. Too late, he tried to unfasten the tiny hooks on her dress, but his precious control had abandoned him, leaving him uncoordinated and his mind disjointed.

Lurai pulled at his trousers, opening them. "However you want," she gasped.

That simple vow severed the last tenuous grip he had on the reins. He turned her, then yanked up on her skirts. The knee-length pantaloons set a torch to his thinking mind. She'd come prepared for polite company, and he was—

"Kar?"

He grasped them, dragging the offending material to her knees. In the next heartbeat, he was sheathed in her body, his hands fisted in the layers of material noblewomen hid themselves inside. Their joining was animalistic, from their sounds to their position and even to their fervor.

For the first time in years, Kar was completely unaware of his partner's state of arousal or climax. He couldn't even calculate how many times he released the pent up sexual energy, let alone how many times Lurai did...if she did.

When he was sated, Kar collapsed to the bed, sweat soaked and gasping for breath. He pulled Lurai with him, holding to the one constant in his life with shaking hands he couldn't explain.

"What ails you, Kar?" she breathed. "Tell me, please."

"What am I?"

Her breathing hitched. "What do you mean by that?" There was something cautious in the response, though he'd said nothing of consequence.

He shifted, finding a more comfortable position on the bed. "You knew me when I was a boy. When did I become a man? Or am I not a man? If I am not, what am I?"

Lurai raised her head, cocking it to one side, assessing him. "You doubt yourself? Why?"

There was no clear answer to that. "The other young men... They are all of a type, all...similar. I am nothing like them, Lurai. What does that make me?"

She stroked his hair back from his face, smiling faintly. "Do you want to be like them?"

Kar considered that. "Not particularly," he admitted. Laysen and the others were awkward, volatile, and somewhat petty.

Lurai's brow furrowed, then smoothed. She smiled. "Do you want them to be like you?"

He sighed. "Is such a thing possible?"

Her laughter was light and lyrical. "Well, not precisely like you, but... I believe..." She hesitated. "Do you trust me, Kar?"

"Of course." Though he didn't understand her, this confusion was immensely preferable to what he'd started the day mired in.

She laid a teasing kiss on his lips. "The barroom you and your friends meet in?"

"The Red Dragon." He worked at her plan, abruptly uneasy. "Lurai, seeing me with you will do nothing to ease the situation." As little as he understood the other men, he was certain of that.

Lurai laughed. "I am certain that is true. Trust me, Kar. Tonight. At evening bell?"

He nodded, watching, dumbstruck, as she righted her clothing, smoothed her hair, and left his room.

"Evening bell," he sighed. Kar just hoped Lurai knew what she was doing.

* * * *

"The absent prince returns," Laysen called out, raising a glass of tura berry wine.

Kar smiled. It seemed his friends had gotten over their upset. He only wished he could do the same with such ease.

Nabin pulled out a chair and waved Kar to it. He accepted the invitation and dropped into it, then motioned the bar for another bottle.

Around the edges of the room, women turned their heads, following his every move. Kar tried to ignore them. Perhaps by doing so, they would be discouraged. It was unlikely, but it was worth a testing.

Nabin's move to speak chopped off mid greeting, and his head came up. Rennel followed Nabin's line of sight, and Laysen was a moment behind.

The soft click of ladies' boot heels in the sudden stillness of the bar announced that there was more than one woman approaching. Kar clenched his jaw at the enticing scent of aroused woman, cursing the fact that the newly regained peace was about to be strained again.

"May we join you gentlemen?"

Kar turned slowly, his head in a spin. Against his better judgment, he chuckled darkly at the sight of Alina in layers of noble clothing.

She raised a hand, offering it to Kar. "My Lord Karliss," she purred. "It has been so long."

He laid a lingering kiss on the soft back of her hand. "It has, Alina." A glance around made his heart stutter. "Lurai, Sulin, Mahree..." Their aim was clear. "Gentlemen, I believe the ladies asked to join us," he hinted.

His friends scattered, pulling chairs from neighboring tables. Alina ignored the one Nabin offered her, folding herself into Kar's lap instead. Sulin took the chair instead, offering blatant flirting to the flustered young lord. Mahree did the same for Rennel, and Lurai bypassed the chair to settle in Laysen's lap.

Rennel dragged his gaze from Mahree, clearing his throat. "You *know* these ladies, Karliss?" His stress of the word was an amusing attempt to ask the question in such a way so as not to offend.

Mahree turned Rennel's face back to her, offering an enticing little kiss as either an answer or a distraction. It was clear the distraction succeeded, whatever her goal had been.

Laysen hissed out a breath, his pupil's dilating. Apparently Lurai had done something overtly sexual beneath the table, most likely played at his cock through his trousers. She leaned around him, either whispering in his ear or nibbling at it. Laysen dropped his head back, swallowing hard.

Sulin was face-to-face with Nabin, trading deep kisses.

Kar's wonder at the whole thing was cut short by Alina's breath on his cheek. His mouth went dry, and his cock surged up. Fire God, but his moments with Lurai felt like weeks ago.

"So ready for me, Kar."

"You know I am."

Her lips teased at the corner of his, and Kar turned to her, seeking her agreement to the taste he craved. Alina didn't refuse him, as he'd been afraid she would. The heat between them was scorching.

She pulled away, and he forced his mind to function. Kar was out of control again. What had happened to it? Would she rebuke him?

Alina tipped her head, drawing his gaze to his friends. They were staring at him, expectant, but for what, Kar had no clue.

"Should we, Karliss?" Laysen asked.

He worked at that. What question was he asking?

Rennel leaned toward him. "They've invited us to..."

Kar glanced at Alina, then around at his friends, Lurai's plan clear as a Frial snow crystal. If his friends had more experience, they would be more like him. "Yes. Yes, we should."

* * * *

Kar smiled at the soft bodies nestled to his. If there was one thing he'd had too little of for his tastes, it was women in bed with him while he slept. The priestesses rarely offered such a thing.

The previous night had been an orgy the likes of which even he'd never experienced before. It seemed every priestess concubine in the temple had come to play with Kar and his friends.

He lay in the bed, savoring the priestesses waking around him. One by one, they leaned over him and gifted him a kiss, then left the bed. Most of them donned a waist wrap before wandering away. A few left in the nude.

His hunger seemed to have run its course. It was not that the sight of them did nothing for him, but his control had reestablished.

Alina remained the longest. She trailed her fingertips over his erect cock. "My mouth or my puss?" she offered.

That simply, his body demanded her. Kar took several deep breaths. This wasn't the time. "I should see to our guests," he managed.

Her smile lit her dark eyes. "Very good, Kar." Her hand retreated. "When they withdraw, you will have me."

He shivered in restraint, laid a kiss on her lips, and stood. There was a male waist wrap hung over the footboard, and he donned it. Alina donned her own and took his arm, accompanying him to the meal set up in a private dining chamber.

His friends were strangely silent, pensive, the nervous energy a fog in the air. Laysen and Nabin looked up at his entrance. The former went wide-eyed...then averted his gaze. The latter stared at the waist wrap as if scandalized by the sight of Kar wearing such a thing. A moment later, Rennel joined him.

Kar settled at the table, Alina at his side. "Did you enjoy your evening with the priestess concubines?" he inquired, his heart pounding.

Laysen reached for his goblet, nodding. "Yes. Thank you, Karliss."

He smiled, relieved though they were unsettled by something. "Do not thank me. The priestess concubines give only what they wish to give."

Nabin mumbled his response into his goblet. "They give so freely."

Lurai ran her hand through his hair. "I would be willing to give again," she offered.

He choked on the wine and then turned to her, his gaze hot. Without a word, he took Lurai's hand and followed her away. One by one, his friends did the same, each with a different woman than he'd started with.

Kar watched them wander away, startling at the feeling of Alina's hand on the fastener for his waist wrap. Something told him that none of their families would see them before evening meal.

SECTION THREE
MELTING THE ICE QUEEN

CHAPTER NINE

"Prince Elgin," Kar greeted his uncle, taking a seat near the window that overlooked the rolling meadows of Aidalyn, their capital city.

It was Furian custom that only the heir apparent to the throne was addressed as "prince;" though Jaygin, Kar, and Kev were all princes, they would be addressed as "lord" until such a time as they were named heir apparent to the throne.

He allowed himself a moment to enjoy the view, swallowing down his longing in a near-painful move. He'd spent the last thirteen years tutored by the priests of Magmon at Magmalen, a largely hedonistic life that included only a few hours of real instruction every day. The rest of his time was spent in little or no clothing, not that they were needed in the tropical south, only a few hundred hectar north of the volcanic ring.

Being summoned to the temperate north, as close to the polar Frial nation as he typically was to the seat of fire, was bad enough.

Being required to wear the clothing of a proper Furian lord was downright stifling. He hadn't worn the cotton tunic for more than five straight days since he'd been fifteen and he'd lived in Frilan's Notch, at the join of the tropic zone and the temperate; he hadn't missed it. He'd never worn the heavy woolen jackets and cloaks required of Aidalyn in his life, and he wished he'd never been in a position to do so.

You are spoiled, Kar! he admonished himself. Still, he longed to run the fields, stripped to as few clothes as he could bear in the colder climate.

You would freeze!

Worse, there was the little matter of his health. Kar had been denied the capitol, in his youth, out of concern that the clime would kill him. What would it do to him now, if he were so foolhardy as to tempt Magmon's ire by dancing around underdressed in the chill air?

Prince Elgin smiled wearily, a sure sign that he expected a less-than-enthusiastic agreement to whatever favor he was about to ask of Kar. If it involved spending more than a week in this stifling clothing, he was right about that assessment.

How will I lead, if I cannot adjust to this form of dress? Perhaps that had been a portion of his father's concern all along. A king couldn't lead from a palace in Frilan's Notch or Magmalen. It went against tradition. Of course, Kar had been balking tradition all his life.

"My thanks for your coming, Karliss." He sighed, settling into the plush chair behind his desk.

"The summons made no mention of a choice in the matter." Nor had Elb, the high priest of Magmon, given him time to prepare and travel in leisure.

The lack of a reply put Kar's nerves on edge. The birthmark on the back of his left shoulder burned hot in warning.

"Uncle?" he questioned.

"The cen-centenial of the Great Alliance approaches."

"I know it." Who could not know such a thing? They'd planned the celebration for the last decade, a lavish festival held every dec-centenial, all the more splendid because it was the cen-centenial. The Frial nobility would attend, of course. Kar was required to attend; Elb had promised a traditional costume for him, hand-sewn by the priestess concubines.

"Every dec-centenial, we hold a—"

"Yes, the festival. Uncle, I know it. Why are you speaking to me as if I were a first-year student? Boys of seven know this."

Elgin darkened. "There is a tradition at dec-centenials, a renewal of the alliance."

Kar nodded. "I know we celebrate it, but there are no records of what the negotiations entail." He'd searched for them, interested in how an alliance could stand so long.

His uncle opened his mouth as if to speak then shut it again.

Realization left Kar cold. "No. You cannot be serious. I am no ambassador. I am not trained to negotiate an alliance." In truth, he was trained for little more than swimming, soaking the sun, eating, and enjoying the pleasures of women. The three languages he spoke could hardly be of use in negotiation, since no one but the priests and he spoke two of them. And the general knowledge and history he knew gave no clue to what his job might entail. There was no time to learn the skills he'd need in the three weeks remaining before the festival.

"It is not a negotiation...precisely," Elgin offered carefully.

"Then what is it? Precisely, now, Uncle," he challenged.

"Their leader—"

"The Ician? She is given a new title every dec-centenial. The... Magmon sear it, I cannot remember the title, but it only lasts for the length of that office-holder. The next is titled Ician again."

"The He-Attalia."

"That is right." And there was a male called the He-Atal, but there was nothing noted about him but his title. Perhaps it was her consort or husband.

"I thought you had been taught this," his uncle fumed.

Kar smiled at that. "The priests seem to try to teach me the whole of general knowledge, a bit at a time. Since they will not tell me what my birthmark means, I scarcely know where to direct my attention."

"It *means* you are to be presented to the Ician."

He breathed a sigh of relief. "Presented? Thank Magmon for that! Whatever the protocol is, I can be trained in time to—" His heart stuttered at the look of exasperation on Elgin's face.

Kar searched for any explanation, but he couldn't seem to find fault with what he'd been saying. "What *is* the protocol?" he asked.

"There is not a precise—"

"Stop! I am a man, not a child. What in Magmon's fire do you expect from me?"

"It is not I that expects it," he grumbled. "It is the Furian and the Frial."

"Uncle," he warned. Why could Elgin simply not get to the heart of the matter and be done with it?

"For twenty-eight years, the priests have forbidden anyone who knew it to tell you what your destiny entails. Now that the dragon's smoke warms your neck, those bastards ordered me to tell you. I ask you, why should it be me?"

"Tell me what?" he demanded. His head pounded in the coming of a sick ache. He'd wanted to know his destiny for as long as he could remember; now that Kar was about to hear it, he suspected he'd want no part of it.

Elgin hesitated, grimacing. "Did you enjoy the priestess concubines?" he asked.

Kar stared at him, trying desperately to follow the chain of conversation in any logical way. "Should I not? What man would not enjoy trained women to share with him sexually?"

"Or the younger Lady Renald?" he hinted.

His face darkened. "Rostana is none of your business!" he shouted. Magmon, how did his uncle even find out about the Aidalyn lover he'd taken a year earlier, at the urging of the priestesses? Rostana had only lasted a few months, but she'd been more than enjoyable while he'd had her.

Elgin ignored his warning, forging on. "Seducing such a woman could not have been easy."

Not as difficult as you think. Noblewomen come south to shed these stifling clothes and find sources of heat aside from the weather; they come to the temple and find a scantily dressed member of the royal—

"She is the Lady Tiben now, mother of Lord Gabel's second son."

"Then she got what she wanted." He furrowed his brow at a faint memory. No, Rostana hadn't wanted the elder Lord Tiben. She'd come to Kar to train herself for the son.

As if his uncle read something of Kar's thoughts in his expression, he answered. "Not quite, but after you..." A weary smile graced his lips. "No *young* man could satisfy...or so I hear."

Kar smiled at the memories of their time together. *But what has this to do with the Frial leader?* The smile left his lips, and his stomach clenched in understanding. "Oh, no."

"Your blood runs hot, Karliss. Surely, you will not have any problem—"

"Being a Frial concubine?" he asked in horror. A worse possibility occurred to him. "Or are you serving me up into an arranged marriage?" He was third in line for the throne, after all, and soon would be second. His grandfather was in his waning years at one hundred and twenty, and the throne would soon be Elgin's.

"Of course not. Karliss, be rea—"

"Have the priests—"

"No! Now, calm yourself."

Kar took a deep breath, searching for his center, but the priests' teachings deserted him in his need.

Elgin echoed him. "The priests encouraged your sexual exploits. Not openly, of course, but they had to indulge your heated sexuality in any way you required."

Kar winced at the unspoken rebuke that he'd required a lot to keep him sated. He supposed there was a payment due for every entertainment; he'd simply never had to pay it so directly before, though Rostana had pushed him nearly to his limits.

"How many women have you seduced, Karliss?"

More than a few. "I am supposed to seduce her? Just that?"

"That is all the tradition requires of you. You will be presented to the Frial court and the Ician tomorrow eve."

"They are already here?"

"You have only the quarter hour before you must leave, Karliss. If you wish to be prepared—"

"I do. I wish the priests had told me this long ago." *How could they do this to me? Why would they?*

"The Ician are raised at a distance, discouraged from showing emotion, discouraged from forming relationships."

Kar smiled in spite of himself. "She is virginal, then?" Magmon, he would enjoy that. Besides Rostana, he'd had only one of the type in his otherwise varied life, and that one had been a young priestess concubine in training.

"She is frigid, Karliss."

"Wha..." He had to have misheard. Magmon could not be so unkind. *I have said my prayers and observed the rites. How have I offended you?*

"Frigid. All of the Ician are."

"Then how can their line continue?"

"The first of each generation from their line is born marked."

"As I was born marked."

Elgin didn't respond to that accusation. "It may be a niece of the Ician in power, a cousin...perhaps. I understand that it is usually a niece."

"Frig..." He couldn't force himself to say the word. How appalling a concept!

"Only the Ician who becomes He-Attalia ever—"

Kar groaned. "*I* am the He-Atal that only appears as a name and no description of his duties? Was it to keep me ignorant of my purpose?"

"Only the priests can answer that. But, Karliss... You need only—"

"Seduce a frigid woman? Are you mad?" Just the thought of it made him ill. "What if I bed—"

"No. She has to be seduced. I have been told..." A look of pain settled on his face.

Kar's blood ran cold. "Told what?" What worse was in store for him? *No wonder Elb didn't want to do this himself.*

"That it is impossible for her to have sex unless she is aroused fully to it."

"Impossible?" he scoffed. "Any woman is capable—"

"Lord Karliss, we await you."

Kar winced at Elb's voice. As usual, the man had come upon him as silently as a snake. "A moment, Elb, if you would."

"Lord—"

"A moment!" Kar calmed himself as the priests had taught him. One did not shout at or order about the high priest of Magmon Himself.

Elb seemed unfazed by the outburst. "Of course, my lord." The door clicked behind him.

Kar rubbed a hand over his eyes. "What am I doing?" He hadn't lacked control on this level since he was eighteen.

Elgin chuckled. "The fires burn hot in you, Karliss. Elb would cast a blind eye or deaf ear to nearly any that prove what you are."

"The fires burn hot, but do they burn hot enough to melt a woman of ice and stone?"

His uncle's smile faded. "The traditions say they do."

Kar rose slowly, smoothing his tunic. "Let us hope the traditions speak the truth."

CHAPTER TEN

"You are mad," Kar grumbled. He rubbed his hands up and down his bare arms, half-expecting to see his breath circling before his eyes. He curled his toes in the rug, dreading the walk to the ballroom downstairs.

He'd thought stepping from the coach, wrapped in a cloak and two layers of wool to cut the whip of the arctic wind, had tested his limits to the extreme, but that wasn't enough.

The presentation was upon him. That meant spending the evening in nothing but a pair of soft suede trousers, padding barefoot on cold marble floors, shirtless in the underheated room air.

"You complained about the added clothes," Elb teased. "Now you complain about the lack of them. You are still wearing more than you ever did in Magmalen."

"I will freeze as solid as the polar ice."

The high priest chuckled.

"You are a heartless bastard. You do know that, do you not?"

"I?" Elb feigned innocence.

"Raising me in Magmalen when you knew this frozen waste I would have to come to. Why did you not prepare me for this?" *For any of this?*

"I did prepare you," he answered cryptically.

Kar grumbled several curses, shifting uncomfortably. He hadn't even been afforded underclothes beneath the trousers; his cock lay, pressed to his lower belly, cradled in the disconcerting glove of the trousers' design.

As if I will be seducing her within minutes of meeting her. A frigid woman?

Elb smiled wickedly, enjoying Kar's discomfort far too much for his physical safety. "You will soon be warm."

"The ballroom will be warmer than my quarters are?" he asked hopefully.

"I imagine not, Lord Karliss."

Kar scowled at him. "Should I dismiss you now?" he threatened.

Elb laughed outright. "I must present you. That much is tradition."

"Afterward, then. *Immediately* afterward." He stepped off the rug, wincing as the temperature of the bare floor sent shards of pain up his legs. Kar forced a calming breath.

I have to acclimate. I must enter the hall a man and not a sniveling child.

"Meet the Ician," Elb interrupted. "After that, tell me you wish me to go." He shrugged. "And I will comply with your wishes."

A knock at the door announced an end to their time to prepare. Elb walked to it, opened it, and passed through, trusting that Kar would follow him.

Kar did what was expected of him, striding down deserted corridors, his arms swinging at his sides in a false show. His chest and arms were stinging already. *At least my feet will numb soon.*

The two priests who'd accompanied them motioned for Kar to stop in the corridor, and Elb entered the ballroom without him.

Elb's voice boomed out in Seh, the language of the gods. Kar wondered at that. Who but the priests and himself would understand it? Or did others speak the language, and he'd never been told it?

Magmon, the god of fire, motion, radiant energy, destroyer of life, yet giver of life... His polar...

Kar bit back a harsh laugh at the pun.

...opposite, Frilan...stillness, patience, barren alone...

His smile disappeared. Was the Ician to conceive from this encounter? Not telling him was beyond cruel.

Kar muttered along with the rest. "She cools his restless fire." Her palace alone had managed that. "He melts the ice queen's frozen heart."

He snorted at that, earning him an exasperated look from one of the priests. Kar ignored the warning.

The Ician's heart had nothing to do with what he had to melt. How many affairs had Kar had? Too many to begin counting, when one considered the priestess concubines in addition to townswomen and noblewomen. Seducing a woman didn't mean love was involved.

Elb switched to the standard language. "Ladies of the court, I present to you Lord Karliss Furia, touched by the hand of Magmon, the He-Atal."

The priests waved him through the doorway, standing back in the corridor to allow him to enter alone. He wondered at that, but the urge to get this farce over with was stronger than his curiosity.

Kar strode through the doorway, forcing his mind off of the discomfort of leaving the square of marble he'd warmed by trying to analyze what was wrong in

Elb's introduction of him. He hid his shock well, as the answer became all too clear to him.

The small room was full of women, about twenty noblewomen and twice that number of priestesses. There was not a male face or form in sight, save Elb's. Then again, the Ician wasn't readily apparent to him, either. If he was to be presented...

Elb didn't address the Ician. Was she not in attendance? Their customs made no sense.

He joined the high priest, nodding to a knot of noblewomen on the way past. "Why are there no men present?" he whispered, hoping for some guidance.

It seemed Elb was once again not of a helpful mood. An arched brow was his only answer.

Kar met the eyes of one woman after another. Would he have his pick as mistress when his duty was done? Or perhaps a different one to warm his bed every night? With shy of three weeks until the festival, it was nearly a perfect match for the number of noblewomen present. They had noted his "restless fire," after all. And did not one accommodate honored guests?

Pretty giggles and whispers made it clear that they knew his mind well enough. One by one, they fell silent, blushing, tearing their attention from Kar and focusing instead on a spot behind him.

He turned, noting the arrival of the Ician from behind a painted screen.

There was no question that the woman was she. Were her regal bearing and stiff posture not proof, her snow white hair and ice blue eyes, pale skin and blue-painted lips and nails could indicate no one else. While the other women wore heavy dresses to ward off a chill, the Ician wore a form-fitting sheath of night blue, sleeveless, revealing the gold bands on her upper arms, slit to mid-thigh on both sides.

Kar was abruptly sweating, overheated even in the chilled air. The urge to strip off the trousers and walk naked, as he had in Magmalen, assaulted him. Adding to that wish, he was hard and aching. Visions of thrusting between her pale thighs had him harder still.

But first, he had to melt the ice queen.

* * * *

Diama considered the Furian male presented to her. His hair was red as embers and his eyes a smoky color between black and gray. His skin was flushed with color, tan but with red undertones, as if he really were aflame.

He was giving off a tremendous heat that she wanted to shrink from. She held her ground despite it. Diama didn't want to become something she was not, but this was her duty, the renewal of the alliance.

His member thickened, lengthening until it nearly pushed out the waistband of the low-cut trousers. That was supposed to fit in her? She was curious to see how.

Well, there was certainly no putting this off. "Welcome, He-Atal. We are honored by your presence."

"Kar," he countered. "Or, if you insist, Karliss."

"Pardon?" she asked, confused by his insistence on such a thing. He was He-Atal; she was Ician, soon to be He-Attalia.

He advanced on her without her permission to do so, grasping her writing hand in both of his. She watched, breathless, as he brought the hand to his lips, forcing herself not to cry out when it felt as if he were scalding her.

Diama swallowed hard in the realization that her personal priestesses had left her back, abandoning their positions of protection and forcing her to face him alone.

Of course. They will hardly hold my hand when he ruts on me.

"What is your name?" he whispered, his dark eyes intent, as if they shared some glorious secret...or soon would share one.

That would be a first; Diama had never had a confidant to share secrets with, had never had secrets to share. How could she in the communal structure of the palace? Beyond that, it was forbidden that she do so.

His eyes begged an answer to a question she had no clue the reason of. What difference did her name make?

"I am Ician. Surely, you—"

"Your name," he insisted. "Not your title. Your name."

She forced herself not to look to Shellia for guidance. Diama was Ician, and she'd been trained to decide for herself, without the interference of the high priestess of Frilan. "What purpose have you in knowing—"

Again, he interrupted her. "When I spend in you, I will not be calling you by your title, Ician. When you scream my name in passion, you will not be using mine."

Diama wrenched her hand from his, appalled at his presumption. "I will do no such thing," she vowed.

The He-Atal's lips pulled up in a strange sort of smile. "That was a challenge."

"Which means what, He-Atal?"

"Kar."

She refused to repeat his name, just because he ordered it. He was a royal, but she was the Frial leader. Both were gods'-chosen to their paths. She was not his lesser in any respect.

He nodded. "A man with my restless fire enjoys a challenge."

"I am pleased I amuse you," she countered, her dislike of the man growing with each passing second. *The Ician not cursed to the year of the dec-centenials were certainly missing nothing.*

He stepped closer to her, blocking every other person's view of what he intended next. The He-Atal pulled her hand up, pressing it to his swollen member beneath the cover of his.

Diama felt an odd flickering in her heart rate and a tingling in her hand. What was he doing to her? Was she changing already?

"You do not amuse me, Ician. You enflame me."

"Any woman would," she replied simply, inexplicably stung by the concept.

"Not any woman. Not anymore."

Her emotions, usually so ordered and sensible, rioted. How dare he say such a thing! "You are an adept liar, I see," she commented coolly. "I shall endeavor to remember that."

She turned to leave, but Shellia blocked her way, her bearing womb coming into contact with Diama's quivering belly.

Shellia bowed her head respectfully. "Pardon, Ician, but there are traditions to be—"

"Have Magmon's Priests escort their He-Atal to his quarters. I will join him there shortly." Perhaps a cool soak in her tub would right her jangled nerves.

"Of course...but if I may be so bold—"

"As if you are never?" she asked wearily.

"Kar is *your* He-Atal, Diama."

"Diama," he repeated, a tone not unlike awe in his voice.

She shot a look of frustration at Shellia, noting the high priestess's amusement with thoughts of physical violence. Shellia had given the He-Atal Diama's name against the Ician's wishes.

Years of lessons coursed through her mind, offering counsel Diama didn't want to heed. There were no secrets in the Ician's palace...not from her and never ones she herself harbored. Still, that didn't mean Diama was forced to speak on every occasion, did it? If Shellia thought it did, the priestess had a surprise in store for her.

"You are dismissed, Shellia."

A smile lifted her lips and she cleared the way to the private corridors behind the Ician's screen. "As you wish, Diama."

* * * *

Kar moved with Elb, hardly noting the hand on his arm guiding him, the priests joining them in the corridors outside the ballroom, or the soothing cooling of frozen palace against his burning flesh. He'd expected the effects of the Ician to fade when she walked away from him, but they hadn't.

The hand left him, and a door closed.

A cloak settled on his shoulders, and Kar pushed it off, growling. He was incinerating, and that fool was layering clothes on.

"He is fine," Elb ordered. "Leave him."

"Fine?" Kar croaked, his mind clearing enough for him to recognize the rooms he'd been given. "This is fine? I have no idea what I am doing and why, Elb."

The high priest's laughter fueled the fire and raised Kar's body temperature yet again.

"Why am I saying these things, Elb? What is happening to me?"

"Oh, so you *do* need me," he taunted.

"Magmon sear your soul, you know I do." It felt like Magmon was searing his own soul.

"You would know it," he conceded, his smile disappearing. "Sit. Please, Lord Karliss."

"I feel as if every muscle is jumping," he complained, turning to pace. "How can I sit?"

Elb gave him no choice. He appeared before Kar, settled his hands on Kar's shoulders, and pressed down, forcing him to the lounge behind him.

"Think of her," the high priest instructed.

"All I can think of is her." Magmon, but it was true.

"Remember what the priestess concubines taught you."

"Let every sense awaken to the woman you are with," he mimicked their words. "Give yourself up to the act."

Kar closed his eyes, picturing Diama as he'd seen her in the ballroom, blue eyes glowing in anger. His muscles unclenched, and he allowed the priests to ease him back on the lounge.

"Much better," Elb urged him. "Do not fight it. Follow Magmon to your destiny."

"I still burn." It was maddening, like being trapped in the southern volcanic ring with no hope of rescue.

"One does not embody Magmon without feeling his power...and his hunger."

Kar nodded dumbly, accessing the ancient stories in his mind with excruciating slowness. "In the beginning, the world was naught but fire and ice. Magmon ruled the south and Frilan the frozen north. Between them lay a waste."

"Good. You were listening."

"I will feed you Magmon's fire personally," Kar snapped.

Elb fell silent in a rare show of a sense of self-preservation.

"Magmon was impatient and intemperate. He wanted dominion over all in the world, so he spread north to the edges of Frilan's lands. Just as I have entered Diama's domain."

"Go on," Elb prompted him. "Finish the story."

"Magmon's heat melted the edges of the great ice plains, and the outpouring quenched the closest fires. The pure waters of Frilan's bounty, coupled with the rich volcanic soil of Magmon's breast, created a lush and fertile land between them."

Kar opened his eyes. "Is she meant to conceive from me?" If so, what would become of the child between them?

Elb sighed. "Only the gods can decide that."

He nodded, strangely comforted that he hadn't been brought to her as nothing more than a stud animal.

"Karliss," he began.

"Diama should be here soon. You should withdraw."

"How far should we withdraw?" Elb asked seriously.

"To your rooms. I may have need of your counsel again."

He bowed his head. "As you wish, Lord Karliss. And if I may speak my mind..."

"As if you never have?" he repeated Diama's words to her high priestess, wondering if all of the gods' most chosen were this infuriating with their charges.

"I am honored to be of service to one who carries the mantle of Magmon so well."

The priests turned as a unit and left him, closing the doors behind them.

Kar wiped the sweat from his brow, cursing Magmon's flame. If this was bearing it well, how had the others thus cursed fared?

He considered his options for only a moment. Keeping Diama off balance had worked so far. Perhaps he would be best served with that plan of engagement.

CHAPTER ELEVEN

Diama strolled through the corridors, in no hurry to reach the He-Atal.

His voice echoed in her mind. *Kar...*

"No," she grumbled. He was not Kar, not Lord Karliss Furia. He was He-Atal, and despite Shellia's opinion, he wasn't *Diama's* anything.

Her "relaxing soak" had become a recitation of Diama's duties, delivered by the thrice-dismissed Shellia. There was simply no stopping the woman when it came to this subject.

It wasn't as if Diama didn't know her duty. She'd been raised with it from the moment of her birth, suckled at the breast of a priestess before her mother's own. Reminders were wasted on her; she'd served her people well and would continue to do so when the He-Atal was gone from her life.

At his door, she considered knocking. Diama rejected that almost immediately; this was her home, and she'd go where she wished, as she always had.

Her greeting stuck in her throat, and she stopped halfway through the door.

Kar lay out on the silk lounge, his head back and his eyes half-closed, as the gods formed him and no more. The fingertips of one hand stroked along his length.

"Diama?" he questioned her.

She turned, slamming the door shut, taking a calming breath...then a second for good measure.

"Diama," he invited.

"Have you no shame?" she asked.

"Is that what they have taught you? That the gods' gift is shameful?"

Diama shook her head. No, she'd never been told that. If anything, they'd tortured her with what a gift she would find the He-Atal, if she allowed herself to see him as such.

"I cannot seduce a woman who determines to be distant. Do you intend to refuse your place as He-Attalia?"

"You know I cannot."

"I imagine you could try." There was no taunt in that. His voice was low and soothing.

She'd considered refusing the tradition, but to what purpose? Failing in her duty to renew the alliance? "I cannot," she repeated.

"Then come to me."

Diama forced herself to turn, mindful that she was Ician, touched by Frilan as she slept the womb, a leader from birth to the grave.

He hadn't moved, save to raise his head and train those smoky eyes on her.

His stillness invited her examination of him. His skin was tan all over, uniformly and to every fiery hair.

"Is that your normal coloring, or do you soak the sun as the gods made you?" she asked stupidly.

His laugh was full of some dark meaning she couldn't comprehend. "I soak the sun in the nude," he confirmed. "The temple at Magmalen affords me a rooftop garden in which to sun and swim."

A strange squirming played at her stomach. "Do you not worry that someone will see you?"

"The priestess concubines enjoy watching me. From time to time, they've enjoyed joining me."

"The priests of Magmalen allow such a thing?" Shellia would have had any man's heart who'd dared watch Diama bathe. Of course, no man could get so close.

"They've encouraged it," he confided. "After all, a man of my hungers...and with my purpose is not stifled in his appreciation of bodily pleasures."

"They raised you?" she asked. "As Frilan's priestesses... I mean... Surely *not* how I was raised, but..."

"Only from the age of sixteen. Until then, I lived with my family and attended the royal tutors. I had only the additional tutoring with Magmon's priests to eat into my days, priests who came to my home after their devotions."

"You know your parents?" She ached at the thought of such a gift.

"Of course. I passed Autumn holidays with them only seven weeks ago." His smile faded. "You never did?"

Diama shook her head. "The Ician are taken from their families a season after birth. For that long, I would have shared the breast of my birth mother and those of every lactating priestess. It encourages the mother's milk to dry painlessly."

"And makes certain you can form no bond of the act." That seemed to anger him.

She stared at Kar, uncertain. "In what... In what way would communal feeding do such a thing? Nay! In what way would solitary feeding *form* a bond?"

His smile returned, and his member twitched. "You are not ready to accept that lesson. Come to me, Diama. Let me seduce you slowly."

Her feet seemed frozen in place. "How slowly?"

"We have nearly three weeks," he reasoned. "Any period of time up to that mark is possible."

She nodded.

"It will take longer, if you will not come to me."

Forcing one foot in front of the other had never been so difficult. It seemed an eternity before she sank to the lounge next to him.

He raised her hand, stroking the muscles in her palm in a way that made her knees shake. "There are not legions of men, Diama. It is only me. It will not be a random cock thrusting into you..."

She gasped as a trickle of water wet her thighs.

"It will be mine." Kar raised her hand to his mouth and pressed his lips to her palm, his eyes searching her face. "Only mine."

Diama stared at the aforementioned member. It was nearly as long as her forearm and as wide around as the exercise bar hung in her room.

"But we will know each other before it comes to that."

"Know?" His words made no sense to her.

Kar turned her face back to his, then drew her down over his chest. "You are so cold," he whispered, stroking his hands over her cheeks.

"It is said you will warm my blood," she replied. Suddenly, that wasn't as frightening as it had been only an hour earlier.

"You certainly heat mine."

"You need warming?" He made no sense. He was the one destined to warm her, not the other way around.

"No, but you do it just the same...in a way no woman has."

Diama sighed. "I do not understand you."

"Is any one person different for you than any other?"

* * * *

Kar waited for her answer, at a loss to explain it any other way.

"Well, you are very different than the priestesses and the nobles," she imparted.

"In what way am I different than the nobles you know?" He wasn't as stiff and formal as most royals and had been compared to a lesser noble many times...fondly. Perhaps the Frilan nobles held to social mores he did not. She did seem shocked by his nudity in his own rooms.

"You are male, of course."

"Surely, you have male nobles," he argued.

"They are not permitted within the inner sanctum of the palace."

"You have never judged one?"

"Many times. Nobles and lowborn alike."

He nodded, prepared to force her to make comparisons, person to person, if that was what it took to make the differences apparent to her.

"When there are males to be judged, I sit behind the screen you saw this eve. It was moved from the audience hall for the event of your presentation."

"Why? Why do you hide yourself from men?"

"It is tradition. They may not look upon me. In fact, you and your high priest are the first men in my lives since my birth father to set eyes on me. You will remain so until we leave for the celebration of the cen-centenial."

"What about social occasions here? Men must attend. Do you spend the entire time behind a screen?"

"You attended one. Men are not welcome for the precise reason you noted. Why should I spend what should be a night of celebration behind a screen?" She seemed confused by his questioning.

"You have truly never met a male." That complicated matters. "Do any of the Ician?"

"No. As I said, it is tradition."

"Very well. Women, then. What woman stands out from others for you?" He remembered the styles of clothing that separated the nobles and priestesses. "Not clothing, Diama. The women within them...and not fleeting differences like who bears at the moment."

She seemed to consider that carefully. "Shellia...the high priestess."

"Good. In what way is she different than the others you know?"

"She is infuriating."

"When she gave me your name?" he guessed.

Diama grimaced at that, then nodded.

"I cannot seduce the Ician as He-Atal. I must seduce Diama as Kar." Seduction was a personal thing, even if it wasn't an affair of the heart, and Diama's innocence was fast engaging his heart.

"I do not understand you," she repeated.

119

"You are more than the title you were raised to be, Diama."

"I will be, you mean...when I am He-Attalia, touched by Magmon."

Kar managed a strained smile, wondering how touched by the god she would be, considering the fact that Elb all but proclaimed Kar was channeling the god onto the face of the world. "No. You are that woman now, Diama. You simply do not know it."

"How could I be?"

"Every step in your upbringing has been structured to deny you the opportunity to learn who you are."

Her breathing hitched. "And what would I learn?"

"That you have always been different than the other Ician were." *Or, perhaps not, and they have always been denied themselves.* "That you have wants but cannot name them, because you have always been denied knowledge of what you truly want."

"What do I want?" She moved closer, as if answering her own question.

Kar guided her lips to his, nuzzling them, nipping at them lightly. Diama didn't respond; nor did she stop him.

He pulled back, staring at the smudged lip tint in satisfaction, knowing he showed the event in a similar manner. Teaching Diama was going to be sweet torture.

Her eyes were strange and far away. "That was a kiss," she breathed.

"Of the most basic sort." Kar traced her lower lip with the pad of his thumb, purposely smudging more of the blue cosmetic. "Do you wish a more involved kiss?" he offered.

Her eyes widened, and she pulled at his arms, indicating her wish to be loose. He released her, letting her leave the lounge. Diama stood, her arms wrapped around her stomach, trembling.

Kar forced himself not to follow her. She had to be *willing* to be touched, at the least, in order to be seduced.

"Return any time, Diama," he invited her in his most soothing voice.

"You want me to leave?"

"No, but your reaction indicates your need to. If I am incorrect, I invite you to stay."

A pained look settled on her face and then was gone. She shook her head, all but bolting into the corridor and shutting the door behind her. Her running footsteps faded away.

* * * *

Diama paced her rooms, shivering. It was cold. *She* was cold. She couldn't recall ever feeling cold before. Was she ill?

That was unlikely. It was more likely Kar's influence on her. Would she have to wear wool dresses and cloaks, as the nobles and priestesses did? Or perhaps the ancient furnaces would have to be lit for her comfort?

The other women would certainly appreciate that. She'd seen their grimaces at the temperature the palace was maintained at for Diama's comfort.

It had been hours since she'd left Kar, and she could still feel his kiss, the kiss that had made a wreck of her cosmetics. That kiss had also caused a disconcerting wetness to form between her thighs, a wetness that had become an icy sheen on her skin before she'd returned to her rooms.

And the pain! Dear Frilan, why had the priestesses not told her there would be such pain involved in a seduction? They spoke only of pleasure. Had they lied or really not known?

Her mind was in turmoil. It was a good thing that all judgments had been canceled until after the festival. There was little question that she wouldn't make good choices in this state.

Is that what leaving him was? A poor choice? Would I have felt pain had I made a different one?

Sending Shellia away when she'd tried to give counsel after Diama's return from Kar's rooms had undoubtedly been a poor choice. Diama had kept the door locked, a lock she'd never used from the day she'd moved into her permanent rooms at the palace until this very day. She'd refused the high priestess entry, hiding her disheveled appearance, though other priestesses had seen her on the mad dash from his rooms to hers. Even now, Diama hadn't applied her powder and tints again.

Memories of her lip tint staining Kar's lips made her ache deep in her belly. Thankfully, it wasn't the tearing pain that had seized her when she'd fled his arms.

Frilan, why does the memory taunt me so? I am not certain I like Kar. Why do I desire him? That is what this ache is, is it not? The ache of desire Shellia has so often spoken of?

There was no way to know, unless she sought out Shellia or another priestess and asked for more knowledge. She wasn't ready to do that yet. She had to order what she did know first, most of all what she knew of Kar.

Assuming the Kar of their last meeting was true, he was a much more appealing and patient man than she'd assumed him to be at the presentation. But how could one know for certain what was real when dealing with a man who possessed so much more experience than she at the art of relationships between men and women?

Shellia trusted the Furian. She trusted Kar...or so she claimed. But, why did she? Why did she trust them within the inner sanctum without even setting priestesses as guards?

There was no way to know that, unless she asked. Perhaps, if Diama understood the reason Shellia trusted the Furian, she might be able to reason her way to that same trust.

Diama sat at her mirror, powdering her face lightly, lining her eyes with the deep blue that matched her dress, then spreading the lighter blue on her lips. Each move was economical, a matter of rigid training that had started at the age of ten...more than half a lifetime ago.

Appropriately presented, she rose and ambled to the far end of her personal corridor where Shellia's rooms beckoned. At this time of night, it was likely she'd find the high priestess at prayer or some craft within.

A laugh from inside stopped her with her hand on the knob. It wasn't that Shellia didn't laugh; rather, the laugh wasn't feminine.

Curious, Diama eased the door open and slid into the semi-darkness beyond. Candles were lit behind the partition that separated Shellia's prayer nook from her bedroom and the ritual bath beyond. Diama peeked around the partition, swallowing a gasp at the scene within.

Shellia lay, tangled in her bed coverings with the Furian high priest. Their mouths were joined in a hard open-mouthed kiss, her fingers fisted in his dark hair and his hands trailing over her body.

His mouth left hers, and his hand circled Shellia's midsection, again and again. Diama did gasp at that, at the realization that he was caressing the babe inside her. Was it the priest's child, then? It wasn't a question one typically asked a priestess of Frilan, the father of a child she carried.

Her gasp was hidden by Shellia's moan of delight.

"No matter what happens between them," the high priest vowed.

"I cannot promise such a thing," Shellia pleaded. "If Diama needs me—"

"Then I will stay here. Kar rarely needs me...or any of the priesthood."

"If Diama allows it. I can promise no—"

He stole the rest of her anguished answer in a kiss, releasing her on an upward slide of his body that had Shellia arching against him, her pointed nipples uncovered in the air that Diama now knew to be cold.

"Remember how our child was conceived," he whispered. His body moved back and forth over hers.

Inside hers. Was this what she would experience with Kar?

"I remember. I remember," Shellia panted.

"Your nightly visits to my rooms in the outer ring. By Magmon and Frilan both, I lived for them. It is not enough, Shellia. Here or in Furia, I must be with you."

"I do want that, but—"

The priest captured her mouth, muting her cry. Their mouths meshed, their kiss slowing and deepening, the high priest's hand laid over their child together.

Diama slipped away into the corridor, more confused than ever. Watching had stirred something in her that Diama couldn't name.

Kar's words echoed in her mind. *"You have wants but cannot name them, because you have always been denied knowledge of what you truly want."*

Did she want what Kar offered, then? It was possible, but the reminder that Kar could still choose to leave her cooled her somehow. She was suddenly less chilled; Diama couldn't say if that reassured her or frightened her. If Kar chose to leave, would it be worth learning and then losing him in the bargain?

I do not even know that I like him. I may be relieved when he is gone.

Still, the drive was there, the urge to know what a kiss would feel like, what Kar's kisses would feel like if she allowed him to become more involved. She shivered both in need and in the chill air, heading to Kar's rooms.

* * * *

Kar looked up from the Frilan poetry book in his hand in surprise as the door opened. He smiled at the sight of Diama slipping into his rooms again.

"Do you ever knock?" he teased, setting the book aside on the quilt beneath him.

She stopped, glancing at the door, closing it, then turning to Kar. "Should I, in my own home? And you said that I was welcome any time."

The painted doll face, coupled with her confusion, was a delight to him. Kar chuckled, waving her closer. "You are most welcome, and it is your home," he conceded.

Diama crossed her arms over her chest, hiding the tightening nipples from his gaze. "Do you ever dress?" she countered, seemingly peeved at him.

"With your nearness to warm me? Should I?"

The question seemed to confuse her further.

"Did you come for a reason, Diama?"

For a fleeting instant, he would have sworn on Magmon's fire that she darkened in a blush. Then it was gone, and the doll mask was in place again.

She cleared her throat and straightened her spine. "You offered..." Diama shot a quick look at the door again, as if she was considering leaving, then sighed.

"Diama?"

She crossed the room to the bed and sat, leaning over him, her breath teasing his lips. "How do you kiss your lovers, Kar?"

Magmon and Frilan both be praised. "Lay with me."

Diama planted her hands on his shoulders and swiveled her hips to draw her legs onto the bed. The motion trapped the bulk of her skirt beneath her, baring her right leg nearly to the top of her thigh.

Kar laid a hand on her knee, noting—as always—how cool her skin was to the touch. Diama nodded her approval, and he slid his hand higher. Her lips parted slightly, and her eyes fluttered closed.

Never one to waste such an invitation, Kar nuzzled her lips wider and then sealed their mouths together. He stroked his tongue along her lips from the inside in preparation for what a lover's kiss entailed. One did not startle an untried woman with an abrupt tongue thrust into her mouth.

Diama groaned, but she didn't pull away. She repeated his move, and Kar rewarded her by tracing her tongue with his at the buffer zone of their joined mouths.

Her body pressed to his, and Kar turned her so that his mouth pressed down on hers, closing his eyes in pleasure. Diama's tongue surged into his mouth, and he joined in the dance. Kar wound his fingers in her hair, tipping her head further into the kiss, feasting on her mouth as she feasted on his.

Cool hands slipped down heated flesh from shoulders to chest, down the line of male curls to his aching cock. Diama's mouth left his in a gasp, then returned of a purpose to carnal knowledge.

Kar released her mouth, nibbling along her cheek to her ear. "The mouth is not the only place I kiss my lovers," he rasped. *Frilan, have mercy! Let her agree.*

"Kiss me as you would a lover," she pleaded.

He sucked her earlobe in, working the line of hooks down her back one-handed. Kar stripped the silk down her body, trailing his lips behind. His cock slipped from her fingertips.

Her breasts were soft and lush, her nipples responsive. Kar sighed at the feeling of her fingers in his hair, her bowing back forcing her deeper into his mouth, and the taste of salt on her skin.

She was sweating; her skin was warming against his. It seemed she'd given herself up to seduction.

Kar slid the silk over her hips, caressing his lips down her stomach.

Her voice was low and sultry. "I see how feeding could form a—" She cried out harshly as he yanked the dress over her bare feet and spread her legs wide.

Her slit wept her honey for him and Kar licked at it, stopping in shock at the sensation of ice against his tongue. He eased back, running his fingertips along her rigid slit in understanding.

Until she is aroused enough, she is literally frozen shut. Elgin was right. She cannot simply bed a man. Seduction is the only way she is able to bed.

Diama moved abruptly, sitting up and scooting back on the bed. Before his eyes, the sweet musk she'd wept crystallized, turning to ice on cooling skin.

"Dear, Magmon," he breathed.

She winced, wrapping her arms around herself, curling her legs beneath her, shivering uncontrollably.

Kar grabbed up the quilts, scrambling off them to collect them all to her body. He wrapped them around her, rubbing his hands up and down her body in an effort to warm her.

Her trembling subsided, and she relaxed into his arms. "Better," she breathed. "Thank you."

"Dear Magmon," he repeated. "I had no idea. Are you in pain?"

"Not now. Only..."

"When the seduction is cut short?" he suggested.

Diama nodded.

"You experienced this earlier, as well?" he asked, horrified that he'd caused her this twice in a single day.

She murmured an affirmative, surrendering to sleep.

Kar wrapped his body around hers, accepting the discomfort of the heat radiating back from the quilts as she'd accepted the freezing rebound of his seduction.

He couldn't do this to her again. The next time he played with her, he'd have to make her transformation complete.

CHAPTER TWELVE

Diama stretched, pushing against the quilt, then pulling it close at the first whispers of frigid air. If this kept up, she'd have to start wearing woolens in the corridors.

An arm closed around her hip, and she went still in understanding. She'd spent the night in Kar's bed.

That meant she had no clothing but what she'd worn in, and that had lain crumpled on the floor all night. Worse, she had no way to reapply her cosmetics. Walking the corridors in such a disreputable state was inconceivable; she'd not done so since she was ten years old.

"Diama?" Kar's voice was a rumble against the back of her head.

"I am feeling much better," she assured him, though she had no idea what he was asking of her.

"You are still shivering in room air," he noted.

"I believe I have begun the transformation."

"Then we should complete it as soon as you are willing," he decreed.

Her heart stuttered and skittered. "What do you mean?"

Kar drew her to her back, a pained expression marking his blue-stained face. "I will not cause you the pain of breaking the seduction again. Do you wish to endure that a third time."

"No," she admitted. "Twice was more than enough, I think."

He nodded. "When you wish to try again, we will."

"Until then?"

He stroked a finger along her lower lip, his eyes soft and far away. "I believe we should make use of my bath."

"Together?"

"Yes. Together."

She hardly knew how to answer that. She'd shared the communal bath with the priestesses, when it suited her to have company, but they were women. Diama suspected a bath with Kar would be a much more intimate experience.

"Diama?"

"Perhaps I should return to my rooms. I have no clean clothes."

"Wear one of my tunics, if you have need of something."

"And my cosmetics—"

"It means something?" he questioned. "The cosmetics you wear mean something?"

"It is tradition. The Ician is never seen without—"

"Then do not apply it again." It wasn't quite an order, more like a strong suggestion.

Diama sputtered for a moment, aghast at the idea of such a thing. "I must, Kar. I have been seen once already without... Perhaps, I should summon Shellia and have her bring them to—"

His jaw tightened in what she could only assume was anger. "You are not Ician," he insisted.

"I am." *Of course, I am.*

"Are you? The Ician has walked these corridors in comfort. Can you?"

She couldn't and they both knew it. Her head ached in the complexity of this situation. If she wasn't

Ician and wasn't He-Attalia, what was she? Was she anything? Nothing?

Kar's hand cupped her cheek, a wry smile curving his lips. "What cosmetics will you wear when you are He-Attalia?"

"I... To be honest, I do not know. I was never trained for it. Perhaps there is no tradition for it. Do you have a tradition for what you must wear? For clothing, I mean."

His smile was stunning. "Only for formal occasions. Try wearing nothing for a bit."

Her cheeks heated, and Diama pressed a hand to them, stunned. She was blushing? She never blushed. *No. The Ician never blushes. Kar is right; I am not Ician.*

"It is all a mask, Diama."

"I do not understand you," she managed. But she was starting to, and his meaning made her brutally angry. Not with Kar but with those who'd raised her this way.

"The traditions, the rules, the cosmetics, the... I admit that I like your form of dress."

"I may have to retire the dress," she admitted miserably. Diama couldn't decipher if she liked the dress or if she simply liked that Kar liked it. She'd never thought about it before.

"To the point, all of those are shackles, trapping you within the identity they forged for you as Ician."

She stared at him, weighing his words. She couldn't dispute them, though she felt something of a traitor for sharing his obvious disgust at the idea of it all.

"Bathe with me," he invited. "Let me see the real Diama."

"And if it turns to seduction?" She secretly hoped that it would.

Kar swallowed hard. "It will not, unless you wish it to. But if it does, we will not stop. You have my vow on both."

* * * *

Kar smiled at her over their dinner plates.

Diama was a different woman without her cosmetics and silk gown. It wasn't the plump, crimson lips and pinked, slightly-pale skin. It wasn't the sight of her long legs protruding from beneath one of his winter tunics or the white hair knotted into a horse tail behind her head. She was smiling and blushing often, talking in an animated manner, more at ease than he'd ever seen her.

The bath hadn't turned into a seduction, but only because Diama hadn't made a move toward it. The sight of her true face appearing from beneath the mask of ruined cosmetics, the feel of her skin behind the cloth he wielded, and the press of her body against his in the tub had had him on the edges of a true seduction with Diama playing the part of an initially-unwilling—in words if not in action—seduced.

Diama's voice broke him from the arousing memories he didn't need if he meant to keep his vows to her...and he did. He reminded himself another half dozen times that he did mean to keep them.

"When the celebration is over, what will you do, Kar?"

He stared at her, noting the way she studied her half-eaten food, pushing it around the plate aimlessly. Unsure what she sought with the question, Kar decided to follow his heart. If Magmon was leading him, forethought and conscious deliberation would likely be the wrong choice.

What did his heart tell him? As the dreams of them the night before attested, Kar wanted her for longer than the seduction. Though he'd balked at the idea of being a Frilan concubine or even being thrown unwilling into an arranged marriage, now that he knew Diama, Kar knew he wanted that choice, wanted that reality. But would she accept him?

"Do He-Attalia take holidays, Diama?"

Her hand stilled. "The celebration *is* a holiday."

"Must you return immediately?"

"What else would I do?"

"Go to Magmalen with me."

Diama met his eyes, perplexed. "What would I do in Magmalen?"

"Soak the sun as the gods made us, swim...enjoy the pleasures we can find in each other."

She moved her gaze to the plate again. "And when our time there ends?"

Kar set his plate on the bedside table and considered how best to phrase his intent. She was frightened by something, but he had no idea which possibility she was frightened of. "You have to return to lead your people," he ventured.

Diama nodded, the plate wavering slightly in her hand. Kar took it and set it atop his.

"Is there a place in your palace for me, Diama?" he asked, his heart aching at what she might say. What would he do if she rebuffed him? Could he give her the traditional night and no more? The craving for her at that thought was no less. He would give her whatever she allowed him.

"You wish to stay?" she whispered.

"If you would allow it." She would have to allow it. If she didn't, he would be banished to Magmalen...or at least Frilan's Notch again.

She looked up, tears dotted on her lashes. "No He-Atal has ever chosen it."

"Diama?" His heart pounded hard in his chest. Did she expect him to leave or want him to?

"I believe there will always be a place for you, Kar." She eased to her knees, leaning across the space between them, her lips finger-widths from his own.

"That is a bold statement. Perhaps, you should sample our passion first," he breathed.

"Perhaps, we both should."

* * * *

Diama tilted her head as Kar had taught her to kiss.

"Are you ready for this?" he asked. "Are you ready to complete your transformation?"

"My entire life has led me to you, Kar. I could not be more ready."

He pressed his lips to hers, urging them open, teaching her a slower version of the deep kisses he'd used on her the evening before. Her body, already warmed slightly, soaked in Kar's radiance as he liked to soak in the sun's.

In moments, the tunic that had barely sustained her comfort all day was too much. She pulled at it frantically, groaning at the discomfort of the bead of sweat winding down her back.

Kar eased her hands away from the fabric, making a sound of soothing in response to her grumble of frustration. "Slowly," he instructed.

"I am burning alive," she complained.

The heat his body gave off, the heat she'd used as a furnace since she'd awakened, beat through the tunic like a bonfire set too close to camp. It was a phrase she'd read and heard spoken of, but she'd never understood it until now.

He worked the tunic up her body, ducking his head to run his lips up and down over her appearing skin. Diama wiggled her arms out of the sleeves and wound her hands in his hair.

"Remove it," he invited.

She uttered an unladylike series of curses and raised her hands from his hair, ripping the tunic off and throwing it as far as she could. Kar's head was lower when she buried her hands in his soft hair again. The lips that had moments before been teasing at her breasts were at her belly, raising quivers inside her.

Memories of his breath and tongue against her seam turned the quivers to outright quaking. "Yes," she urged him. She didn't know the words to ask for what he'd done before, but she trusted that he would know her mind.

He tarried, tasting all of her from throat to knees, waking nerves long dead to sensation. It was maddening, and yet she wanted it never to end.

When he finally reached her slit, she was wet and warm, laid back beneath him, raising her hips to beg for more silently. There was no discomfort in the stroke of his tongue as there had been the last time. Her flesh wasn't rigid and resisting. It moved with Kar's attentions, parting to his tongue as her lips would at his urging.

Just when she thought there could be no greater feeling in the world, he moved higher and captured a bit of her flesh in his mouth, nearly bringing her off the bed in response. Kar paid painstaking attention to it, licking in intricate patterns, suckling it until it beat at her nerves, nibbling it lightly so she cried out for more.

Still, he continued. Kar drove her on, until Diama felt certain she might go mad.

The abrupt crumpling sensation inside had her gasping in surprise. A pulsing pleasure that spread from it, bringing a drugged weakness to her limbs, was followed by an inferno of need for something she couldn't name. She gasped out pleas for an end, for more, for understanding of what was happening to her.

Kar's training served him well. In an instant, he was over her, his upper body braced up on his arms, the crown of his member spreading her slit with torturous care.

A sudden realization assaulted her, that his length filling the conspicuously empty space inside her was what she needed. "Now, Kar. I need all of you." There was no embarrassment in the numb calculation that everyone in the rooms along his corridor likely heard her demand it. There was no room for such petty concerns in the firestorm of their joining.

His thrust sent her body into a riot. Was it pleasure? Pain? Pain so acute it was a pleasure in itself. He was hot, searing, and her body rose to meet it, physically and in gradients of heat. The scream filling the air around them was her own; her throat felt raw in the effort, but she could hardly recognize herself in it.

The only clear sensation was a hunger she'd never felt before, clawing at her. As if Kar felt it, too, he moved within her, hammering strokes that matched the drum beat of want.

Diama held to his shoulders...then to his hips, with no memory of moving her hands from one to the next. She pulled at him, demanding more, her fingers curling reflexively as he complied.

His seed coursed out, buffeting sensitive tissues, touching corners even his deepest thrusts hadn't. She pulled at him, lost in the cascade of pleasure again. Their cries rang out, melding in the air around them.

But there was no peace for her, even in what she assumed was the climax the priestesses had described to her. Diama still burned, still craved what he could offer.

"Feel the fire," Kar whispered. "Use it. Open yourself to me fully."

"I have. I will again." *And again...and again.*

"Nothing exists for me but you. Allow the feeling to take you." His voice brushed along nerves that were raw, a touch unto themselves.

Her hips rose and fell, cycling against his still-erect length. Diama didn't fight it, letting her body rule her mind.

"Yes," he urged her.

Kar rolled to his back, bringing her with him so that Diama straddled his hips. She didn't question what he was doing; the position allowed her to take what she wanted.

CHAPTER THIRTEEN

Kar opened his eyes, smiling at the feeling of Diama wrapped in the shelter of his body, her soft buttocks pressed to the tender length of his well-used cock.

He'd never felt Magmon's fire so clearly before. For the last three days, they'd rarely slept, rarely eaten. They'd been so immersed in each other that priests and priestesses had come and gone unnoticed in the midst of their passion or, less often, their sleep, collecting nearly-full plates of food and leaving fresh, leaving an assortment of clothes and cosmetics that lay untouched.

Elb hadn't told him it would pass this way. For the first time in his life, Kar was thankful for the gift of his silence.

Diama shifted against him, and his cock hardened in pleasurable pain. He'd thought their marathon had ended when they'd slept the night, but he wanted her still.

Her sharply-indrawn breath announced that she was awake and aware of him, eager to sheath him again.

"Open for me," he requested.

She slipped her hand between her thighs, parting her slit for him. Kar eased in, sighing at the fact that Magmon's full force had been burned out at last. He took her in slow, gliding strokes in deference to their abused bodies, and still they flew to a kinetic release.

In the aftermath, they lay together, panting in exhaustion.

Diama spoke suddenly. "I believe we should hold an audience," she stated.

"The nobles will see us presented at the festival," he replied wearily, fighting off sleep again.

"Not for the nobles. There is something I must see done."

"As you wish."

* * * *

Kar stood to the left of Diama's throne, a step behind, his hand on her shoulder. He wasn't certain what she intended, but he would support her.

Magmon's fire still burned hotly enough that they dressed sparingly. Kar wore the traditional suede trousers, and Diama wore a crimson dress in the style of the one she'd worn as Ician. She'd stripped off the blue nail tint and put on a soft pearl pink. Her lips were glossed but not tinted, and her face was otherwise free of augmentation.

Elb and Shellia entered the ballroom together, bowing their heads, then waiting for whatever announcement was to come.

Diama's voice was strong and sure, the sign of her years as a ruler. "The Temple of the Silent Moon will be changing, Shellia."

The high priestess furrowed her brow in confusion. "In what way, He-Attalia?" She was being formal, most likely thrown off guard by the strange pronouncement.

"The southern wing will now be home to a group of Magmon's priests and priestesses. My husband should like to celebrate the Fire God as he always has...nearly." A smile curved her lips at that.

Kar mirrored it. "You know I have no wish for the priestess concubines," he assured her.

Diama continued. "Having been touched by the Fire God myself, I should like to know the proper rites for his praise."

He resisted the urge to tease her that she was learning them quickly and was an adept student. The high priestess's rising upset stayed his tongue on that comment and prompted another from him.

"As I wish to know Frilan and give her thanks." He resisted the urge to ask Diama why this confrontation was necessary, lending the appearance that they'd reached some accord between them.

Shellia took a calming breath. "The temple is to be shared between the gods, then?" she inquired carefully.

Diama nodded. "With you leading Frilan's priestesses there." She turned her head, motioning for Kar with her eyes.

He took in the direction she indicated from the periphery of his vision and then spoke, hoping he was interpreting her move correctly. *Why did you not simply tell me what you wished me to do?* "I trust you will stay on as my personal priest and advisor, Elb?" Kar stated it as if it were a foregone conclusion that the high priest would abandon his post in Magmalen in such a manner.

Diama's smile confirmed that he'd chosen correctly, and Kar nodded, thanking Magmon silently for it. His wife took the floor again.

"Since you have worked so closely with Shellia, I am certain the two of you could create balance and harmony of this arrangement."

Elb appeared shaken, but he nodded. "I believe we can."

"And The Temple of the Silent Moon lies just outside the palace grounds. You will be close enough to act as advisor to Kar."

She turned to the clerics again, seemingly considering more. "None of the He-Atal have chosen to stay before," she mused.

Kar wondered at that. He knew she'd considered that fact closely. Why would she act as if it surprised her?

Shellia offered a weak wave of her hand. "None of the Ician have felt Magmon's fire as acutely as you have," she ventured.

Which explained why the clothing left for Diama ranged from the sheath she wore to woolens. They had no way of knowing, until an Ician emerged from the transformation, how she would be affected by it.

Diama broke him from that line of thinking, her voice ringing out again, sure as she hadn't appeared moments before.

"When He-Attalia bore in the past, their offspring were consecrated to Frilan."

"Should they not have been?" Shellia's voice was tense to nearly a challenge of that statement.

"Of course, they should have," Diama dismissed her. "But... Kar is staying, and I *have* been more deeply touched by Magmon than they have."

Kar hardened at the double meaning of her words.

Elb cleared his throat. "You wish to consecrate your young to Magmon?" he asked, sliding a glance at Shellia that showed his discomfort at the thought was as strong as the high priestess's likely was.

"To both Frilan and Magmon," Diama corrected him. "I believe all children of dual parentage should be likewise consecrated."

Shellia and Elb stared at each other, seemingly deliberating something silently.

Kar winced. *The plan to bring our nations closer is already crumbling.*

Diama's voice broke the moment of tension. "Starting with your own. When *is* your child due, High Priest Elb?"

Shellia paled, placing a hand over her swelling womb, and Elb wrapped a steadying arm around her. Kar swallowed a laugh, his mind locking on Diama's game, at last.

Elb managed a tight smile. "Less than a season," he answered her.

Diama smiled. "Your first visit," she calculated. "I wondered why it took so many visits to *settle things.*"

Shellia darkened to crimson. "He-At—"

"I know of your secret promises, Shellia. If I did not approve of them, would I have arranged to keep you together?" Her smile disappeared. "Or do you wish to go to Magmalen as High Priest Elb wanted? I would release you to it, if that is your wish."

"N—no. I prefer to stay here. This is my home."

Elb nodded his agreement. "I told Shellia that I would stay if you wished her to stay. She would never leave you, whether she claimed she would or not. I have always known that."

"I know," Diama replied slyly. "I have heard it with my own ears."

"Diama!" Shellia protested.

"It is my home, and I did hear a man in your rooms," she excused herself. "I was curious."

"When did you...hear such a thing?" Shellia was nearly purple in embarrassment.

"The night of the presentation, long after you left me to consider your words. It did not take me long to unravel why you trusted them so."

The high priestess opened her mouth as if to speak, closed it again, and shook her head. "Diama...you kept a secret."

Diama covered Kar's hand with her own. "I had already been touched by Magmon...or, at that time, by Kar."

MAGMON'S LOVER

PROLOGUE

Lady Rostana Renald stood at the side door to the temple, her heart beating wildly. She reached for the bell rope, touched it, and retreated.

Surely, this was a joke. But she didn't walk away. The question was whether her hope that it was true was enough to overcome her terror that it wasn't.

She touched the rope, not quite forcing her fingers closed around it. Rostana could learn if it was a joke or not by pulling it.

If it is, the embarrassment would be more than I can bear.

If it is not, I may yet have Zaden as my own.

On that thought, she squeezed her eyes shut, yanked the bell rope, and released it with a wince at the too-loud jangling.

The few moments between that move and the sound of someone behind the door were enough to trigger the need to run. Dragon's Breath, how would she explain her presence here?

Just as Shara told me to. She gave me the words to use.

The door swung open, leaving Rostana face-to-face with a bare-chested man in red trousers. Was he a servant in the temple or a priest?

He assessed her for a moment, then bowed his head. "Welcome, mi'lady. How may I serve you?"

Rostana didn't want him to serve her. She wanted Zaden. *Magmon sear his frustrating hide!*

It is the only way. But I must speak the words, as Shara spoke them. "I...come from the wastes with the gods' own hunger."

He quirked up an eyebrow. Her heart sank, and she started to turn, muttering an apology for wasting his time.

"Come. Please. If you hunger, you have come to a place of satiation."

Her heart skittered in surprise and excitement. It was the response Shara had told her to expect. Rostana nodded and followed him through the corridors. He stopped at a red drape, drawing it back and waving her through.

Terror rose up in her, and she froze. That was the whole of it? Shara had led her to believe there was more to it than the passing of words and the man bedding——

"Mi'lady?" His voice was soothing. "There are formalities to be met."

Formalities? He wasn't rushing her to a bed. Rostana nodded and slid through the doorway, sighing in relief at the very mundane office beyond. Trembling in the release of tension, she took the outside chair and folded her hands in her lap.

He took the other. For a moment, she feared he'd reach for parchment. If he did, she would leave. It would be mortifying to know he'd recorded this conversation.

"Why have you come to Magmon's temple, mi'lady? What...hunger vexes you?"

She knew the words she had to speak, but forcing them out was impossible. Her face burned in conflicting emotions.

"I see." His look was all too knowing. "Wait here, if you please."

The priest left the room, and Rostana chanced a look at his narrow waist and tanned back, at the firm backside inside tight trousers.

She considered leaving. *Magmon sear Shara's soul! This is a sick joke. Why her cousin would choose to play such a prank on her was immaterial. It was unlikely that Magmon's priests were in the business of deflowering young noblewomen.*

The drape moved again, and a most shocking sight appeared. There was little question that the woman was a priestess, but she was like no priestess Rostana had seen before. She was bare-breasted, dressed in a waist wrap even shorter than the ones the native men wore.

Rostana nearly bolted at her approach, but something in her smile was disarming. The priestess offered her hand, and Rostana took it, trying not to stare at the other woman's nudity.

"My name is Alina Senior," she offered. "And you, mi'lady?"

"Renald." High priestess or not, she was a cleric and wasn't someone Rostana would share her given name with.

The priestess tipped her head and moved to the chair the priest had abandoned, folding herself into it. "Lady Renald." Her voice was silken, a comfort to Rostana's jangled nerves.

They stared at each other for long enough to send protestations of a mistake up her throat. They stuck there, forced down by the need to appease Zaden.

"You came here in search of Magmon's touch?" Alina Senior inquired.

That was what Shara had called it, what she'd said Rostana would have to ask for. "Does it exist?" she asked, forcing the words out.

"Oh, it does indeed," she purred in a voice that made Rostana's heart stutter. It so closely mirrored the way Shara had spoken of the experience, it was eerie.

The priestess launched on into a new question. "Have you known men, Lady Renald?"

Flames the likes of the volcanic ring licked up her face.

"If you wish to experience Magmon's touch, you must be honest with me," she warned.

Rostana swallowed hard, reminding herself that there was a price for every service, and she'd pay nearly any price they asked for this one. "I have...touched, Alina Senior."

"Have you tasted?" she asked bluntly.

"Only of a man's mouth and he of mine."

The priestess arched a fine brow at that. "A man's cock has breached none of you?"

She shook her head slowly, praying the priestess wasn't playing along with Shara's prank.

"Has a man touched you?"

A roll of pleasure at the memory settled in her belly. "Yes."

"Beneath your dress?"

"Yes, Alina Senior." Dragon God, but the phantom memories of that touch had her sweating.

"Inside your body?"

"No." Rostana had shied at that.

"Have you been tasted? Beneath your dress?"

"No, Alina Senior, I have not." But she ached for it.

"You seem saddened, Lady Renald. Tell me what drives you here."

"A man," she whispered.

"The one you touched with?" she guessed.

"Yes."

"Tell me why you hunger, if you have such a man."

"He prefers knowing women, ones he can enjoy without the games of induction."

"And so you wish to return to him such a woman?"

Rostana managed not to wince by a narrow margin. "Yes, Alina Senior."

"You wish a man to teach you, to seduce you by Magmon's fire?"

She didn't hesitate. "Yes, Alina Senior. I do."

The priestess seemed to consider that. "Very well. I will show you to your rooms."

"And then?" Rostana asked nervously.

"Go about your devotions. Never forget, Magmon hears all."

* * * *

Kar smiled at the flash of red in the trees surrounding his swimming pond. Since no priest had immediately requested his presence in Master Elb's rooms or offered a missive from his family, Kar could wager with confidence that it was a priestess concubine watching him swim.

The question remains, did she come here to watch or to join me? Just the thought of the later had him erect.

Kar flipped to his back, floating instead of swimming, displaying his state of readiness to the priestess lurking in the shadows, a blatant announcement of the fact that he was ready for any amusement she sought. Either she would disrobe and join him, or she would not. Kar could offer, but the choice to accept lay with the woman in question.

The rippling of water against his skin announced her answer. Kar kept his eyes closed, letting her come to him.

Her body stretched out along his, her lips caressing his side. She nipped at his ribs, most likely a rebuke for not looking at her. Women liked to be the center of a man's attention.

"Do you hunger, Kar?" she teased.

"Alina," he breathed. "How could I not hunger for you?"

He never knew which of the priestesses might choose to join him, but once one had a time or two, he knew what to expect from the joining. This particular priestess had chosen his company dozens of times in his years at Magmalen. She'd come and gone from the temple twice, and she'd only been back in Magmalen for a few weeks this trip, barely enough time to tan her skin.

Alina was one of the high priestesses, a senior. She'd been recently elevated, though she was only three-quarters the age of most high priestesses, only seven years Kar's elder. Few seniors chose to come to Kar once they elevated, and it surprised him that Alina still did so.

Her hand slipped down his chest, then encircled his cock. She stroked him, laughing in delight as he moaned. Kar wrapped his arms around her and then kicked his feet in the water, guiding Alina along with him.

Her nip at his ribs bordered on painful.

"Your meaning?" he inquired. There was always a lesson involved when Alina caused him anything but indescribable pleasure.

"Whose pleasure are you seeking, Kar?"

He felt his cheeks heat at that. She was correct, as usual. He'd been busy contemplating what would get him between her thighs the fastest. He stopped kicking, abandoning the grassy shoreline.

"My apologies, Alina." Would she leave him now? Priestesses had, when he'd lacked patience. "It is a gift you offer me...if you still offer." It couldn't hurt to repeat the lessons she'd taught him over the years back to her.

"Good. The stairs are a good choice, Kar."

She confused him, but he had come to expect that. He kicked his way to the rounded marble stairs he liked to soak the sun upon.

At the edge, he settled his ass on a stone beneath the surface, leaning back on the one higher. Alina took his lead, her wet, black hair a sheet around her body and her dark eyes questioning him, perhaps testing him.

"Open your senses to the woman you are with. Lose yourself in her body's song." Alina had taught him that herself.

There was no question she wanted him. Her nipples were hard and begging for his attention...but not his mouth; her tipped head indicated that she wanted his kiss.

Kar cupped her cheek with one hand, placing the other around the curve of her ribs, just below a pert breast. Alina met him halfway to the kiss, brutally driving his arousal higher. She bowed her back, offering her breasts, giving him the signal to raise a hand to them.

At this point, losing himself in a woman was easily accomplished. Her scents and sounds, coupled with her movements against him, wove a tapestry pattern to bliss one could not miss if he were blind.

That being the case, Alina's abrupt halt was like ice water tossed in the heat of his lap. Not that he was rendered flaccid by the move as he understood some men would be, but it was a shock nonetheless.

"I did something wrong?" Kar asked in disbelief. At this point, he rarely did.

"Nothing," she purred.

He licked his lips, confusion warring with the mind-numbing pleasure of her resumed stroking.

"I have a gift for you," she breathed.

Shudders of Magmon's hunger wracked him. Would she mount him? Perhaps suck him to climax? Invite another priestess to join them?

Alina nipped at his ear. "I know how you love a seduction."

But Alina loved leading him. Seducing her was impossible. A petty corner of his mind questioned how many of Magmon's priests she'd played thus to elevate so quickly. He asked forbearance for such unkind thoughts almost before said thought had fully formed in his mind. He was out of sorts, his bouncing libido wrecking havoc with his mind.

"Such control, Kar."

He forced his muscles to unclench.

Her stroking became more avid. "Your attention to my lessons should be rewarded."

Kar braced his hands on the upper step, his breathing ragged in preparation to spend in her hand. She stopped abruptly again, and he tensed, the pendulum effect stringing his nerves tight.

"Perhaps I should leave you hungering for her," Alina mused.

"For whom?" he managed hoarsely. "A local petitioner or a new priestess?" Either was possible.

"Neither."

Alina parted his lips, her kiss unleashing his raw sexual need. Whoever Alina was preparing him for was going to receive Kar at his most potent edge.

He pulled away, his head spinning. "Who is she? Tell me."

She swung her leg over him, riding the sensitive under edge of his cock. "A noblewoman from the north, Kar. Untried save kiss and touch."

He moaned at the thought of such a gift. "What does she seek?" *Magmon's fire, let it be the same thing I do.*

Alina avoided answering the question. "She is a cousin of Lady Eberly."

Visions of Shara's body swallowing his cock nearly sent Kar to climax. Shara Eberly was no untried maid, and she'd been very enthusiastic.

"Lady Renald believes her cousin sent her here as a joke," Alina confided.

"Renald..." Magmon sear it, he couldn't place why the name was so familiar to him. "What does she wish?"

"What you can teach a young woman who wishes to play in society's games as a senior in experience."

"Magmon, yes." She wanted an introduction to loveplay. She wanted to experiment, to try even the more extreme pleasures he could teach.

Alina slid off his lap, chuckling darkly at his hiss of displeasure. "Go to her, Kar, but remember—"

"Her pace," he grumbled.

She leaned forward at the waist, and her lips closed around the head of his cock. Kar thrust deeper, his control strained. Then she was gone, climbing the stairs, leaving him in agony.

"You will take no other until Lady Renald is properly educated."

The shock of that statement made his blood run cold. "What?" Was she mad? Educating an untried woman for the more involved games could take weeks. Perhaps a month. *Or more.*

Alina paused, her wrap halfway fastened around her hips. She cast him a sly smile over her shoulder. "Release yourself, as you feel the need to, but you are forbidden to take priestesses until Lady Renald returns home sated."

His mind worked hard at that. He was forbidden priestesses, but she hadn't said —

"And you are forbidden to take women from the local bars to your bed...or theirs. Your only lover, for the duration, will be Lady Renald."

"But why?" he demanded.

"Your control is still strained, Kar. A man who lacks control is not a man worthy of the gifts women offer."

"This is training?"

She nodded, fastening the final hook. Alina turned to him, her hands on her hips, her bare breasts still inviting him. "When this test is complete..."

His cock pulsed in response to her tone. "Yes?"

"If you please her, you will be pleased in equal measure."

Kar waited for an explanation of that. He already enjoyed priestesses on a regular basis. What was she promising?

Alina leaned down, breathing the answer to his unasked question in his ear. "A week, Kar. For a week, you will have every priestess concubine for the asking...how you want, when you want...no lessons to break up your days and no refusals."

"Magmon, yes."

* * * *

Rostana ran her fingertip along the marble altar top, cursing herself for a fool. Why had she believed Shara? Chances were Shara had found nothing in Magmalen but a native club with cool drinks and a servant hung like a stallion to have a tawdry little affair with.

The interview for entry into Magmon's temple had been mortifying, and her current state of semi-dress was no better. When she'd been shown to her room, Alina Senior had given Rostana a wrap. Thankfully, it wasn't the short wrap the priestess wore. Rostana's wrap fastened under her arms, instead of at the waist. It extended to just above Rostana's knees, a full hand's length longer than the one the priestess wore. And

Rostana's wrap was brown, not the red that the priestesses and priests wore.

Unfortunately, it was meant to be worn without underclothes. Though women seeking the game went without, they did so beneath layers of dress that would show no sign of it.

Now, more than an hour after changing into the disconcerting costume, Rostana sat on the padded bench before Magmon's altar, staring into the life flame, at a loss for what to do next.

She hardly knew what she should pray for. That Zaden would be hers for the price of this farce? That she would find him lacking and be able to dismiss him as callously as he'd dismissed her? That she would further find someone better?

No. There is no one better for me.

She shook that thought away and considered the final possibility miserably. There was still the chance that this was a joke. What would she do if Alina Senior was, even now, sending a missive to her father, requesting Renald the Elder to come save his younger daughter from herself?

"An interesting way to show devotion," a man's voice rumbled out.

Rostana startled, rising and turning to the heavy drape that served as a door to her rooms. Her knees went weak, and she grasped at the altar to steady herself.

Magmon himself could not have been more beautiful. He was a hand's length taller than Zaden was and so bronze of skin she'd have assumed him a native if not for his red hair. His shoulders were strong and yet she knew, without a doubt, that he wasn't a worker; his hands would be smooth and uncalloused on her tender flesh.

He didn't wear the trousers the other priests she'd seen in Magmalen wore. Instead, he wore the same sort of waist wrap Alina Senior had. Her heart stuttered in the certainty that it was all he wore, as the wrap was the only thing she did.

He didn't make a move toward her, though his expression spoke of concern. "Are you in need of assistance, Lady Renald?"

Rostana shook her head, though her knees wobbled a bit. "Are you... Are you the one Alina Senior sent to me?" *Magmon, I hope he is.*

He raised his hand, offering it to her. When she hesitated, he curled his fingers in silent motion to take it.

Rostana took a calming breath and placed her hand in his. To her surprise, he guided her to the bench and aided her to the surface, then stepped away.

"About your devotions," he began.

"Are you a priest, then?" His wrap was the red the priests and priestesses wore. Perhaps he was.

Perhaps Alina Senior has sent for my father, and this is just another ploy to busy me.

"You may call me Kar."

"As you wish," she replied with a respectful tip of her head.

"What do you know of Magmon?" he asked.

"He is the Fire Father, the Great Dragon, radiant power from whence all life springs."

Kar smiled. "That much, you can learn from a moldy tome in a eunuch hermit's hole. What do you know of His fire?"

Rostana shifted uncomfortably at a man asking such personal information, priest or no.

"When a man touches you, do you feel Magmon's heat searing you, asking to be fed?"

Her cheeks burned at his bold descriptions. "I feel it," she whispered. Why else would she be here?

"Do you bring yourself to the fire? Do you give yourself up to the burn?" he persisted.

"I do." *To visions of Zaden.* But Kar didn't need to know that.

"Then why were you not showing devotion properly?"

Rostana stared at him, shocked by his concept of devotion.

"Have you never heard the saying 'filled with Magmon's fire'?"

"Of course, but I never thought it meant... That is devotion?"

His smoke-colored eyes assessed her.

"You wish me to...bring myself to fire? Here? Now?"

He didn't reply.

"There is no door."

One brow arched. Kar extended his hand to her again, drawing Rostana to her feet. She followed him into the corridor, her nerves jumping.

Kar led her up one floor and back the direction they'd come. He stopped at a heavy drape, motioning to Rostana for silence. Sounds of passion filtered from inside, a very heated encounter she'd guess. He nodded and then turned her back toward her rooms.

The lecture began. "Magmon's fire is not shameful, Lady Renald. Neither is it something to be hidden away.

"No one but myself will enter your rooms without your permission to do so, no matter what they hear."

Rostana stared at him. Would he walk in while she played at her own body?

Fool! If Alina Senior sent him to me, that is likely the least intimate thing he will do.

"I may come into your rooms at any time of the day or night," he warned her.

"And if I am not showing proper devotion?" she questioned.

"No one can at all times. One must rest, eat, bathe, and otherwise occupy the mind and body."

Rostana wasn't certain what he wanted from her.

Kar raised her hand to his mouth and brushed his lips over her knuckles. "I will know if you have shown devotion, Lady Renald."

"I trust you will, Kar."

* * * *

Rostana lay on her bed in the temple, her heart pounding. Why was it so difficult to touch herself here, when she'd done it so many times at home?

She'd like to claim it was the strange place and lack of privacy that bothered her, but she'd be lying, if she did. In truth, now that she'd resigned herself to the fact that others could and would hear her passion, she found she rather liked the idea.

No, her disquiet came in the form of Kar. Though the young priest hadn't returned, visions of him haunted her when she closed her eyes. The guilt of that had stayed her hand. Rostana was doing this for Zaden. What was wrong with her that she was fantasizing of another man?

She pushed that thought away angrily. Zaden no doubt had other women warming his bed in her absence. And Zaden could have chosen to be the only man she bedded. He hadn't chosen it, so it was his fault that she had another man to dream of.

Who wouldn't fantasize about Kar? Just the thought of him entering her rooms...touching her...

The visions were too much for her. She shifted, rubbing her thighs together.

Magmon sear it! Rostana sought out the center of pleasure between her thighs. Her fingers stroked, and her hips cycled. She didn't bother to stifle her cries as she did at home. Perhaps if someone heard her sounds and carried the news to Kar, the young priest would return soon.

Climax neared, and Rostana thrust her hips up, imagining Kar over her, entering her. Her scream of release was earsplitting. Magmon, but she'd never dreamed of venting her cries like that at home.

Her body cooled slowly, her heart pounding in time with the lessening contractions. She listened for sounds of approach, but there were none. Rostana sighed. How many times would she have to show devotion before Kar would return to her?

* * * *

Kar sat in the bed pushed against the other side of the wall where Lady Renald's was. He'd known she'd choose the bed, though he hadn't expected her to take half the day to screw her courage to the task. It was going to be a long seduction, at this rate.

Her voice rose now that she was close to release. If he dared rush her and risk Alina's displeasure, he'd go to her now and finish her with his mouth. Lady Renald was surely so lost in pleasure, she would allow it.

But that defeated the purpose of putting her at ease with her sexuality and introducing her to Magmon's fire. No. He would have to wait.

Her scream of release was as clear as if he'd been inside her when she'd vented it. That thought had him burning for the reality of it.

"Forbidden to take another," he grumbled.

Kar took his cock in his hand, stroking hard and fast, fantasizing about Lady Renald's pretty little mouth gifting him. The fluids leaking from the tip lent to the illusion.

Oh, yes. I will have her mouth, and she will have mine.

It didn't take long to send himself over. Kar cleaned himself with one of the cloths he had stocked for just such an occasion. It seemed he'd have need of quite a few of them.

He settled on the mattress. It wasn't as comfortable as his own, but he couldn't hear her in his own bed. Knowing when she was showing devotion was critical to the timing of his plan of seduction.

CHAPTER ONE

Ten weeks later

Rostana sauntered into the tavern, dressed for the games and intent on her prey. Oh, how times had changed. The last time she'd come through those doors, she'd played prey to Zaden's predator. That woman was no more.

She sighted him immediately, at a corner table. As Rostana had expected, Zaden was busy plying a young woman with passable wine and filling her ears with his promises.

It is time to learn if his promises are worth the energy to utter them.

Something told Rostana they weren't, but she went to him, intent on an answer.

In her months away, she had come to know herself. Moreover, Rostana knew she was more than capable of pleasing a man and being pleased by one. If there was a lack, the cause would be clear.

Intent on the test, Rostana wrapped her arms around Zaden from behind. She leaned to the right, whispering his name against the shell of his ear...then nibbling it leisurely.

His breathing hitched. Zaden turned, probably intent on asking something.

Rostana didn't give him a chance to. She slanted her lips to his parted ones, enticing him into a carnal exchange. Zaden turned in his chair, dragged her into his lap, and pressed her to the evidence of his arousal.

Her hand sure, she stroked him erect between their bodies. Zaden groaned. His lips parted from hers, his breathing ragged. All the while, she took stock of him. He was passably large, smaller than Kar but nearly a match for the other priest she'd known.

His eyes slid open, then widened. "Rostana! You've returned." His shock was impossible to miss.

She smiled at that, adding another blatant caress. "We had unfinished business, I believe."

In the background, Zaden's chosen partner of the evening stood and left, looking more than a little rattled.

Do not despair. Whatever I spread of Zaden and our night together will either save you grief or make him more appealing to you. Something told Rostana that nothing Zaden was capable of would make him more appealing to herself.

He enjoyed what she was doing for a moment, then snapped a look at the empty chair his companion had vacated. His jaw tightened in anger, and his dark eyes narrowed. "What are you doing?"

A chuckle escaped her lips. "I would have thought that would be obvious."

Zaden shoved her away from him. Rostana stumbled, reaching blindly for a handhold. The edge of a table gave her the balance she sought. He came to his feet, towering over her.

Before she could right her senses to promise punishment for such treatment, he was shouting her down. "Why would I want a woman like you?"

Her anger burned hot. "Be careful what you wish for, Zaden. You wanted me educated, but now that experience will benefit other men." She didn't care what man it benefited, as long as Zaden suffered in the knowledge that he'd never taste her passion.

"I wanted to educate you," he grumbled. "I just wanted you open to any experience, not..." Zaden motioned uncomfortably up and down her body.

"You wanted a woman too stupid to know how inept and uneducated you are between the sheets," she guessed. That woman wasn't Rostana. Her lovers would have to be exceptional to live up to the experiences she'd already had with the priest concubines at the temple in Magmalen.

"You are a wanton," Zaden accused.

Her cheeks burned. "How dare you!"

"The only man who would have someone like you is —" He stopped abruptly, his eyes went wide, and he swallowed hard. Zaden's color dropped several shades.

Rostana stared at him, confused by the reaction. She turned, trying to follow his line of sight for some clue to what ailed him — and ran headlong into a male chest nearly at her back.

"What is the meaning of this, Zaden?" The voice was deep in the promise of violence. And more.

Rostana's body reacted to his presence much as it had to Kar's. Whoever this man was, he would be fire unleashed in the sheets. She didn't doubt it.

"Nothing, Father." Zaden's voice had gone tense at the question.

She didn't look at him; Rostana wanted to see more of the man wrapping a protective arm around her waist. *Lord Tiben.* She wished she knew his given name.

He was tall, nearly as tall as Kar was. His clothing marked Lord Tiben as a high councilor, though he appeared young to hold such a position. His hair was as dark as Zaden's, with only a sprinkling of gray above his ears.

Unusual coloring for a native of Aidalyn. One of his parents must have come from the south.

His face was unlined, save the barest crinkles at the corners of his deep blue eyes and his lush lips.

A sign that he smiles quite a bit. That speaks highly of him.

Surely, Zaden's father was younger than her own was. Zaden's grandfather must have been very old when his son had been born or died very young to leave him in such an exalted position at his age.

Rostana rested a hand against his chest, shivering in delight at the hard wall of muscle. *Magmon sear it!* He had the body of a fighter and a lover. Her mouth watered to taste it.

Lord Tiben's gaze snapped down, his eyes meeting hers. "I apologize for my son's appalling behavior." It sounded sincere, which made him all the more appealing.

"My thanks," she managed.

"*My* appalling —"

"Zaden, return home...now. I will deal with this blot on our name tomorrow."

"But —"

His gaze left Rostana, focusing on his son over her shoulder, and his jaw tightened. "Go now, or I will have guards escort you to one of the cells beneath the manor."

She shuddered at the thought of it. No family had used those cells in a hand of generations. They were a holdover from a less civilized era.

Lord Tiben's hand tightened on her waist, drawing Rostana closer to his body. His gaze returned to her face. The cells were washed away as a concern that quickly.

Zaden stormed toward the street, grumbling curses. Neither of them watched him leave. Rostana's breathing was short in sexual awareness of the lord holding her so intimately.

I want him to hold me much more intimately.

"Do you require a priestess healer, Lady Renald?"

She didn't question how he knew her name. "No."

"Be certain. I saw my son's assault on you. He will pay dearly for treating a lady in such a manner. I assure you." Lord Tiben tipped his head in promise of that.

"I am certain." What Rostana needed was someplace more comfortable and private, not a healer.

"If you would allow me," he hinted.

"Anything." The word was out before she could censor herself, and Rostana darkened in realization that she'd spoken it aloud.

His mouth softened into a knowing smile. "My coach is outside."

She nodded her agreement.

He turned, guiding her by way of the arm still wrapped around her waist. It was a blatantly sexual show, not at all the way he'd have escorted her if he'd planned on returning her home without a sample.

Zaden waited for a public cab outside. He snapped his head around, his eyes narrowing at the sight of them together.

Something hard and mercenary rose up in Rostana at that. She hoped Zaden's rooms were close enough to his father's to hear their passion unleashed.

Lord Tiben lifted her into the coach as if she weighed not a thing. He followed her in, sitting close on the wide seat, though there was room not to. Zaden's snort of disgust was cut short by the click of the door being closed by the driver.

"Home," her escort ordered without looking away from her.

Then his lips were parting hers, heated in Magmon's fire, bringing the promise of scorched senses on the sheets. Rostana welcomed it, urging him on, taking his measure in the swaying coach.

* * * *

Gabel pulled away, his head in a pleasant spin already. When she'd blushed, he'd thought his son in error about her experience, and he'd meant to prove her out as a poser and return her to her father with a stern warning about the dangers of the games. But there was nothing inexperienced about Rostana Renald.

It made no sense. All the stories circulating about the woman had her painted a virgin, a prim and frustratingly skittish virgin at that.

Still, the hand stroking him up had knowledge and a purpose. Such things were not learned without long and arduous study on the matter. Study a woman so young was unlikely to have engaged in, especially with bucks like his son as teacher. Rostana had summed up the situation perfectly when she'd called Zaden inept; most of the young men were.

"You have played the games extensively," he guessed. How could she without word passing? Admit it or not, all men listened to the stories of the young, and a woman like Rostana — either the virginal woman of tale or the seductress — would have caught Gabel's attention.

Her blue-green eyes glittered in mischief, then were nearly lost to him as they left the bright lights of the main street and turned down another.

"No. I have trained in...Magmon's fire." Again, a hitch that said she knew less than her body attested.

Trained in Magmon's fire? What in the aforementioned God's name did that mean?

If she wasn't a player, blocks of knowledge might be conspicuously missing...like preventing pregnancy. If that was the case, there was no way Gabel would take her to his bed without precautions, precautions he would have to send Lir out to procure. It had been a long time since he'd lain with a woman who wasn't on a daily herself, and he would not be accused of siring someone else's issue.

Still, he had to know what her odd comment meant. "Who trained you?"

He saw her dark lips curve up in the lamplight streaming into the dim coach. Highlights of red appeared in her mid-range, brown locks.

"I trained at Magmon's temple in Magmalen."

"The *priests* trained you?" If they had, it was an abuse of their power to do so. If they had, the ones responsible would pay dearly for it.

Her brow furrowed in confusion, and she smoothed her hair. "One priest did." She was cautious now, probably scenting that something was wrong.

"Within the temple?" Nothing was secret in Magmon's temple. There were not even doors inside the structure. If one priest touched her, every priest and priestess would know it.

"Of course."

His heart pounded at her naivety. Zaden was wrong. Rostana wasn't a wanton. She was a wronged child, and he had to learn who was responsible for it and make those persons pay.

Before he could ask further questions, she started talking again, clearly agitated by his responses. "He was a priest concubine."

There was no such thing, but hearing it might be too much a shock for her. "Who...introduced you to the priest?"

"My cousin Shara told me to go to the temple and request Magmon's touch. A senior priestess concubine sent the priest to my chambers to teach me."

"Magmon's..." His throat went dry, and the calculations made him dizzy. The cen-centennial was upon them. The He-Atal would be training in Magmalen. Certainly, they would want the God Vessel to bed with innocents, in preparation for what he had to accomplish.

"Mi'lord?" Rostana's voice was unsure.

"Had he a mark? This priest concubine?" Was it possible that she'd been inducted to the love arts by the God Vessel himself, Magmon's hand on the face of the world? If so, his son was a fool to refuse her and a traitor to lay a hand in anger to her. Such a woman was a rare treasure.

"Yes. A hand on the back of his shoulder." She reached a delicate hand to the back of her own shoulder as if in demonstration of the placement. "Is it important?"

Gabel didn't answer her. Instead, he captured her lips in a second searing kiss. The Dragon God had sent this blessing, and he wouldn't waste it. How often does a man get to touch what the gods have?

The coach came to a halt, and Rostana broke away, her breathing ragged. "Lord Tiben —"

"Gabel," he corrected her. "Do you wish to share my bed, Rostana?"

"Oh, yes."

Lir opened the coach door for them, and Gabel lifted Rostana into his arms as if she was his bride. She was precious, too precious to tread on the same streets others did.

Servants opened doors for them, but Gabel had attention to spare for only one person...Rostana, virgin concubine of the He-Atal.

She was young for Gabel, nearly indecently so, but he would have her. He would savor her as she should be savored, as his son certainly would not have in a young man's haste.

The doors to his bedroom shut behind them, and he strode to the bed, setting her gingerly on it. Gabel went to his knees and stripped off her shoes. His hands not quite steady, he lifted her skirts.

Rostana sighed, reaching for him. Her hands were like silk, and her touch like the brush of a bird's wings. Surely, even the God Vessel had been affected by her.

She'd dressed for the games: her silk stockings held up by a garter and no other undergarments to slow them. Gabel sampled her ample musk, groaning as her fingers fisted in his hair.

Rostana rose against him, her hips cycling. He shivered in delight at the fact that she took pleasure in him after laying with a god.

"Gabel." She panted out his name a second time.

He ate ravenously, driven on by the need to bring her to climax. He was a man; perhaps she would find his finesse lacking in comparison to the He-Atal.

As if arguing the thought, Rostana shattered for him. Her scream echoed off the walls, and her cream flowed for him, making his head spin.

Gabel rose up between her legs, watching her chest rise and fall in the aftermath of her climax, her glazed eyes opening and closing again. He stripped off his jacket and shirt, needing to be inside her with an intensity he'd not felt since he'd been a young man, before Zaden's birth, at least.

It is Magmon's fire. He didn't question that it was so. Rostana had come to him, full of the Fire God's own passion, and she was feeding him on it.

Her hands worked at his trousers, and Gabel let her, opening one catch on the back of her gown after another. He knew what she intended, but he couldn't allow that yet. If Rostana serviced him with her mouth, Magmon's fire might wear off before he felt her sheath milking him dry.

Gabel moved, just as her fingers circled his cock, easing her gown down her body to reveal her pert young breasts. At his age, he'd never thought to encounter such a treat again.

Her head rocked back at the first sucking motion against a beaded nipple. His name left her lips on a groan. Rostana pushed her dress down her hips and kicked it away, leaving her clothed only in the garter and stockings.

Gabel stroked at her, working Rostana to a fever he could feel radiating off of her. There was little question she'd been touched by Magmon Himself.

She arched against Gabel, inviting him in. "Please, Gabel."

"Are you on any sort of suppressant?" he inquired.

Rostana's eyes opened, and her brow furrowed. As he'd feared, she'd never considered it before.

"A-aren't you?" Her voice squeaked, and she paled a few shades. "I th-thought men..."

"Young men playing the games often do, but you cannot trust in it." Since Gabel took only sporadic lovers, he used situational preventatives.

She bit at her lower lip, misery etched on her lovely face. "Then we...we cannot —"

Gabel kissed her, working at the problem. Stopping was unacceptable. He drew away. "Promise me anything I wish."

"I am not a wanton," she breathed. Rostana crossed her arms over her breasts.

"You are not. I will make it right," he vowed. Gabel didn't question what he wanted...what he'd intended, probably since the moment she'd shattered to his mouth.

She stared at him, her expression shifting so fast it made him dizzy.

There was one thing he had to know. "Have you taken any man but the priest concubine?" Gabel couldn't risk any confusion over parentage of a child she might conceive. Though it was said the He-Atal could produce no issue until he'd met the challenge of the Ician, the same could not be said of another man she might have bedded.

"Only..." She averted her eyes.

Gabel drew her face around again. "Only who? When?"

"Another of the priests. When the priest concubine was training me. He — he trained me for two men." Her hands fisted against her breasts, and she glanced at him then away, her face going crimson.

His stomach clenched at the idea of the God Vessel using her in such a manner. Had it amused Him to make an innocent play wanton games?

Those questions had no answers. "When? How long ago?" Gabel didn't ask if the other priest had used a preventative; it was a safe wager she wouldn't know for certain. She'd thought all men did.

"A month... A bit more than a month, I suppose. I waited to approach Zaden for..." She motioned a hand, showing her unease with such discussions.

"For your blood to flow and stop?" he guessed.

She nodded. "What does that —?"

Gabel kissed her again. With more than a month, there would be no question who'd sired any child she might carry, and her blood indicated that she didn't carry. "Promise me anything," he repeated.

The heat between them spiked. "Anything," she vowed.

Dragon God's fire, Rostana would be his. Gabel eased her hands from her chest, and she unwound in his arms, opening herself around him.

Gabel pushed his trousers down his thighs and followed her to the mattress. His first thrust brought her hips off the bed and wrenched a scream from her. Her sheath fisted tight around his girth, taunting him with her youth.

Rostana held to him, her hips moving in time with his. Her passion was scorching, bringing up a sweat on his skin and hers. That was all the indication Gabel needed that it wouldn't end with once.

"Come for me," he demanded.

The God Vessel had discarded Rostana as a mere mortal woman, unworthy of His continued attention, but she was more than that. If she responded to Gabel this way, she was fated to be his; there was no other possibility.

As if his order was her breaking point, Rostana shattered around him. Her sweet body milked his over, and she jerked in strengthening contractions at the feeling of his cum coursing into her.

Mine. By the gods, she is mine.

CHAPTER TWO

Again? Rostana's head spun at Gabel's tireless nature. She'd thought older men would wane after an adventure or two, flagging on the sheets. If all older men were like Gabel, the young women playing the games were wasting their time with green boys.

They'd heated the sheets, again and again, never more than an hour of napping before he woke her for more. Gabel's cock was hard and large — not quite as long as Kar's but thicker by far, so thick he stretched her tight around him in every position.

This time, he'd rolled to his back, and she straddled him. That glorious cock twitched against her sensitized nether lips, and she gasped. Oh, yes. This time would be no less exciting than any other they'd shared.

"Do you ride, Rostana?" he teased.

She moaned. He'd teased her thus several times.

"Do you enjoy a man's taste, Rostana?"

"Does my cock satisfy you?"

As if there was any doubt of that. The man was Magmon's hunger unleashed on the world.

"Ride me."

Her body was wet and ready for him. Rostana hissed in pleasure and pain mixed as the crown pushed through sex-bruised rings of muscle.

His blue eyes darkened in passion. In one roll of his hips, he filled her. That simply, her body took up the throbbing drum beat of need he unleashed.

"Yes," he breathed. "You feel it. The rhythm of the ride."

Rostana nodded. She felt it. She needed to match it.

At first, Gabel lay still beneath her, his eyes half-closed in pleasure. Then he was moving, taking her deeper.

His whispered words made no sense at first. Rostana made no effort toward trying to hear them, believing they were empty words of encouragement. Her heart stuttered at the truth, and she struggled to clear her mind enough to take them in.

"You are mine now, Rostana. No man but me will touch you. Not the God Vessel Himself."

It was sacrilege, and yet it made her heart speed in pleasure that he'd said it.

"Say it." There was an edge of command in that.

Rostana didn't hesitate. "Yours," she gasped out. If he could make her feel this way, why would she want anyone else? "Only yours."

As if there was some magic in the words, her body and mind rose in a wave of pleasure, crashed hard on the rocks, and parted in a warm spray. She screamed his name, pressing down hard on his cock, needing to feel every finger width of him filling her.

Fill her, he did. His cum was hot and potent, filling her...overfilling her. She'd always heard men had a limited supply, but that was another tale that didn't seem to apply to Gabel.

There was a sound behind her, but Rostana didn't turn to see. She'd had an audience before. Though her time with Gabel seemed more private than her time with Kar, she didn't care who saw and heard them. She'd promised she was his, after all.

"Rostana?"

She forced her eyes open at the sound of her father's voice. Her muddled mind directed her head around until she met his shocked eyes.

Gabel wrapped the sheet around her body and eased her to the mattress, placing himself between her and her father. "I would speak with you, Renald," he announced.

"I dare say we will speak." There was an edge of anger in that.

Rostana shuddered at the coming scene.

As if in reassurance, Gabel turned and planted a kiss on her forehead. "Sleep, Rostana. If you choose to join me for meal, my robes are in the closet there." He indicated the direction with his head.

She nodded, letting her eyes drift shut, too tired to consider what might be said between the two men.

* * * *

Gabel smiled at the sight of her. Rostana's eyes fluttered shut. She was so trusting, so sweet and innocent, despite the God Vessel's tutelage.

"Tiben," her father warned.

He nodded and rose, collected a robe from the aforementioned closet, and belted it around his body. Then he waved Lord Rojer Renald to the door. If Rostana meant to sleep, she would do so without interruption.

Gabel motioned to Lir, letting him know that a light meal should be set for Gabel and his "guest." The house steward hurried away with a look of relief, most likely that Gabel hadn't offered correction for allowing Renald to barrel past the usual protocols of the house.

The older man didn't wait to be seated at the table. "It is unseemly, Tiben. It is unacceptable. When I heard your son had attacked my daughter, it was bad enough. To find her balanced on your randy, old cock..." Words failed him at that, and he motioned up and down Gabel's body.

Gabel sighed. "Rostana has agreed to be my wife."

Renald's face went a waxy gray, and he gaped for a moment. "I will not allow it. Rostana is too young to make such a choice for herself. She has only just made twenty years. She's only taken one lady's respite."

"And do you know what transpired on it?" It was a safe wager he didn't.

A modicum of color returned to his cheeks, a sign of a father's embarrassment with the thought of his daughter's budding sexuality. "I would imagine she started playing the games. Many young women are more comfortable doing so away from home."

Gabel led the way into the dining chamber and settled at the head of the table in silent show that he was lord of the house. Renald took the seat to his left, a sign of opposition.

When the cup of strong morning tea was in Gabel's hand, he broached the subject. "Rostana took a lover," he offered bluntly. "Well over a month of...instruction in the love arts."

Renald choked on his tea, going red as the piping on a councilor's robes. "Surely not! My daughter is no wanton."

A bit of experimentation with a young buck she might or might not further marry, using a preventative, was one thing. No father would allow an affair; that sort of thing was for bored ladies whose husbands were doing the same and widows. It was the sort of thing Gabel had indulged in himself, from time to time, since his first wife died bringing Zaden forth.

"No, she is not that," he agreed. "If Rostana was, I would not consider making her my wife. She is better than that, by far."

His adversary stared into his cup, seemingly mollified but not by much.

"Do you not want to know?" Gabel pressed.

Renald took a deep drink of the tea, fortifying himself. "What man would do something so dishonorable? I think I should," he grumbled.

"It is not what you think."

His guest's cup hit the table with enough force to send tea splashing to the linens. Lir came running, and Gabel motioned him away. Though he seemed confused by the order, the steward complied, leaving the two lords alone with the rather prickly problem between them.

Renald composed himself. "Who?" he demanded. "Magmon sear the man. Who dared do this?"

"Magmon does sear him," Gabel offered. "The God Vessel Himself seduced Rostana from her virginity and educated her in the fine arts of loveplay."

His jaw dropped. Renald forced it shut, tried to speak, and failed. He shook his head.

"You are the king's man, Renald. You know the sign the priests look for as well as I do, though few do. Rostana's *lover* resides at the temple in Magmalen, and he bears the mark. She thought him a...priest concubine. She has no idea what it means, I am certain, but she has been touched by the Fire God Himself. She burns with His hunger."

He went strangely silent. "And you want her for that hunger," Renald accused.

"I wanted her before I sampled it. But I cannot ignore the signs."

He stared at Gabel, perplexed by something. "What signs?"

"She responds to me avidly, though I saw her dismissal of inept young men in the games. After knowing the touch of the God Vessel, she revels in mine. How high must her standards be? And still, I satisfy her. How few men would please her now that she has lain with a god?"

Gabel expected a protest of that...scoffing. Refusal to let her become wife to a man old enough to be her father.

Instead, Renald nodded. "She will not find happiness in the usual way. Not after such...experience."

"Then you will not fight me? You will agree to a swift resolution that makes her my wife?"

There was a moment of tense silence. "You wish to sire a second heir on her."

His cock lengthened at the idea. "While I am young enough to be a proper father," he admitted. "Rostana deserves such stability in her life. As mother to one of my heirs, she will be cared for, even if I leave her a widow."

Renald didn't reply to that.

"Rostana is precious to me," Gabel admitted. "I carried her into my home as one would a bride, because I could not bear to think of her walking the streets mortals walked."

He nodded. "I will not fight the resolution. How soon will you want to conduct the ceremony?"

"Soon. No longer than a week. "If Rostana's timing was that of most women, she would be fertile sometime in the next week. She would be properly his wife before any sign of his heir resting in her womb was evident.

Renald offered his hand in agreement. Gabel took it, his heart easing.

With a last sip of his tea, Renald rose. "There is much to be done. My wife will expect Rostana for preparations this afternoon. I will get the king's agreement to the resolution today."

"My thanks."

Still something niggled at the edges of his consciousness. Renald was the king's man. Though the identity of the He-Atal was a closely-guarded secret, the king and his advisors would know it. "Who is He, Renald?"

The other man stopped in the doorway, turning back with a raised eyebrow.

"Who is the He-Atal?"

"You know I cannot tell you that," he offered cautiously.

"Is He worthy of Rostana? Besides being the God Vessel, is He?" Though He'd played heinous games, Gabel had to know He hadn't done so because of His lack of position...to spite or snub her.

Renald considered that. "And if I said He was not?"

Gabel considered that. "I would likely always dislike Him, but it would not change how I feel about Rostana."

"He is worthy of a woman like my daughter. Had He offered her a place as His bride, I would not have objected to the match, but we both know that is not in His future."

"Even if He'd offered it as I did?"

Renald's face hardened. "If He had offered it as you did, I would have taken the matter before the king myself."

Gabel laughed heartily at that, relieved for some reason he couldn't name.

CHAPTER THREE

Rostana stretched, blinking her eyes in the late morning sunlight. For a moment, she couldn't place where she was. The unmistakable scent of sex taunted her senses, and a parade of erotic images left her gasping for breath.

Gabel Tiben. Magmon's heat, but the man was sex unleashed.

She smiled. And she was in his bed, nude, wrapped in a sheet, full of his seed.

Her brow furrowed. But he wasn't. *Why isn't Gabel here?*

Her father's face wavered in an exhausted memory. Gabel had wrapped her in the sheet and lifted her from his still-erect cock. There had been tension between the men, but Gabel had demanded they speak.

The fact that she was still here in his bed, hours later, proved that there had been some amicable end to the discussion, but what that end was, she could not say. Especially considering the fact that Gabel had not come back to bed with her.

"Sleep, Rostana. If you choose to join me for meal, my robes are in the closet there."

She pushed from the mattress and hurried to the closet he'd indicated. As promised, there were dozens of fine robes inside. Rostana eliminated the longer ones immediately; they would drag the floor. She settled on a blue that matched Gabel's impassioned eyes and took it to the open bathing chamber.

The bath beckoned, but Rostana didn't want to wait that long to see Gabel again. Her stomach growled, voicing its agreement. That decided, she relieved herself, washed her hands and face, and used Gabel's brush to smooth her hair.

Dressed in the blue robe, she headed for the corridor. A knock stopped her with her hand a whisper from the knob, and she gasped, pulling back.

"Lady Rostana?" a strange man called out.

She pulled the robe tight over her chest and cleared her throat. "Come in."

The door opened, and the house steward entered. He glanced at her, then bowed deeply. "Ah, you are awake. Lord Gabel sent me to wake you."

"H-he did?" Was he angry that she'd slept so long?

"Yes, mi'lady." The steward turned, leading the way toward the stairs. "If you would..."

Rostana forced herself not to hurry. "Of course."

The top of the staircase was in view when Zaden's voice brought her up short.

"So, it is nearly midday, and the wanton arises."

The steward shot an open-mouthed, wide-eyed look at Zaden, then looked away, seemingly ruffled by the heir of the house's rudeness.

It seems the servant will be of no help. Her father's servants were ordered to see to the needs of guests above all else save the whims of the lord and lady of the manor; it seemed Gabel's servants had not been so instructed.

That a given, Rostana ignored Zaden and took another step. Whatever he chose to say, he could say it. After his father's warning the evening before, Zaden dared not touch her.

As if proving he knew his limitations well, Zaden moved between Rostana and the steward, blocking her way. Her heart hammering, she looked up at Gabel's son.

Zaden's nostrils flared, and his eyes were hard in challenge. Rostana forced herself not to step back from him. Though his muscles bunched and released in warning that he was considering violence, she didn't question that Gabel wouldn't stand for another attack on her person, lover or no lover.

That didn't stop Zaden from stating his thoughts. "What are you playing at, Rostana?" He didn't give her time to reply. "Being here can only bring disgrace on both our houses. I'm sure you know that. Yet here you are, seducing an old cock. As I've said before —"

"Lord Zaden," the steward gasped.

"Quiet. This is between —"

"Certainly not you," Gabel informed him.

Zaden turned slowly, giving Rostana a momentary glance at Gabel, glaring down at his errant son.

"I suggest you return to your room and do not emerge until I call for you," Gabel suggested, his voice cold and clipped. It was a voice that promised punishment if Zaden dared balk him.

"Father, I —"

"I know very well what your intentions are. Go. To. Your. Room."

Zaden stomped away, taking only a moment to glare daggers at Rostana. He brushed past her, not hard enough to be called a shove, just enough that his father might overlook it.

He didn't. "We will be discussing that as well, Zaden," Gabel promised.

Rostana watched him march down the hall, his back stiff and his fists clenched. He turned into an open doorway, and the door slammed hard behind him.

His rooms. They would have to be on the same side of the house as Gabel's rooms. That wasn't unusual. The heir's rooms and the nursery were typically the closest rooms to the lord and lady's rooms.

"Rostana?" Gabel's voice was low and soothing.

She turned her head and focused on his outstretched hand. *The steward will see if I take his hand.* Then again, what did it matter? His entire household would know Gabel had carried her in and they'd engaged in their share of sexual games.

Rostana took his hand and allowed Gabel to wrap her arm in his. He escorted her down the stairs formally, as one presented a lady to a group of peers.

He led her to the dining table and seated her to the lord's right.

Rostana wrapped her arms around herself. "Perhaps I should return home."

Gabel sank into the chair to her left — the head of the table. Seemingly unconcerned, he motioned to the steward. When the servant disappeared, he met her eyes and spoke.

"You will."

Her heart ached at his agreement. It was a dismissal. *Of course it is. His heir disapproves of me.*

"You will be returning here for dinner."

Words to reply stuck in her throat. It took several long moments to force them out. "I — I will?" Why would he want her to return when Zaden would make his life akin to the flume of a volcano for it? Upset enough — and there was no question he was — Zaden would start rumors out of spite. Wasn't Gabel concerned about that?

"You will." Gabel motioned the servants laden with food to Rostana, a silent order to serve her before himself.

Her cheeks heated and she stammered out her thanks. *It is not done!* On some level, Rostana was mortified.

The lord of the house was nearly always served first. There were rare occasions when it wasn't so: when the king, a prince, or a high priest came to dine, for instance.

The servants retreated, and Gabel picked up his fork. "You will, Rostana. There are formalities. We must attend to them."

Formalities? Rostana picked at her food, trying to make sense of what he was saying. She couldn't. "There are?"

Gabel's lips quirked up in a smile. "How very innocent you are."

Rostana's cheeks flamed. After the excesses of the previous night, how could he say such a thing?

His hand cupped her cheek. "Delightful," he murmured. Gabel eased his hand away. "You recall your promise to be mine?"

"Of c-c —" She gasped. At last, his meaning became clear. The servants had laid her food first; the lady of the house was served before the lord and heir, when there was such a lady.

Rostana swallowed hard and met his gaze steadily. "My father will never approve," she admitted. Her father was the king's man; if he disapproved, the king surely would.

"He already has approved. Even now, the king affixes his seal on the resolution we need to wed." Gabel waited a moment, then motioned toward Rostana's food.

She started stirring it idly, her emotions in a riot. She was amazed that he'd managed the approval of both her father and the king. Still, there were insurmountable difficulties in the match.

"Rostana?" he prompted her.

"What about Zaden?" She dared not meet his eyes.

"My son will toast our joy or be exiled to our estate in Volcalen." It was a simple, inelegant decree from a lord that expected to be obeyed.

"But people will say —"

"I *know* what they will say." He took her hand and kissed her knuckles gently. "I will right my errant son, Rostana. You will focus on our ceremony and nothing more."

That warmed her heart. "I will," she promised. "I will make it a ceremony to be envied."

"With you as my bride, how could it be anything less?"

* * * *

Gabel closed Rostana into his coach and watched it depart. True to Renald's word, the resolution had been delivered to Gabel before the end of the midday meal. Now his preparations had to begin in earnest — starting with his son.

His smile faded, and he turned to the house. Either Zaden would give his vow to show nothing but support for this marriage or he would be gone by dinner. That thought firmly in mind, Gabel marched to his son's rooms and entered without knocking.

Zaden lay on his bed, his legs crossed at the ankles, his arms folded under his head. He stared at the ceiling, sulking like a chastised child might.

"Is *she* gone?" Zaden's voice reinforced the image.

"Rostana has departed...for the moment."

His son snorted and his jaw tightened. "You mean to soil our name with a public and sordid affair then."

"No. I mean to marry her." Gabel waited for the explosion, counting the heartbeats.

At five, his son shot to an upright position. Zaden paled, then went crimson. His eyes narrowed. "The scandal to demand a resolution alone —"

"I have already been granted the resolution. There was no fight and no scandal."

"Then she is a wanton. Why else would her father allow —"

That snapped Gabel's tenuous hold on his patience. "She is *not* a wanton. I warn you that I will not tolerate that lie from you or from anyone else."

Zaden screwed his face into an ugly sneer. "I heard your sounds, I remind you. All night long, Father!"

"And you will many more nights, I trust." Against his better judgment, Gabel smiled.

It took a moment for his son to recover enough to speak. "They will say you mean to plant a second heir and you are dissatisfied with me. They will say —"

"Undeniably, that part is true." Perhaps a reminder that Zaden was easily replaced would stay his son's hand.

"You mean to replace me?" There was a warning in that, though Zaden had no power to injure Gabel.

"I suppose you have a few decades to mature and prove yourself worthy to be my heir." Gabel leaned against the door frame, feigning consideration.

His son straightened, his expression hard in challenge. "I see."

"I doubt it." Gabel ambled into the room. "I have turned a blind eye to your shortfalls and attitudes. Perhaps I indulged you too much. Perhaps the lack of a mother's breast affected your appreciation of women."

"Father! I —"

"Silence."

Zaden snapped his mouth shut. His jaw tightened another few notches.

"Now..." Gabel took a calming breath. "I trust Rostana will raise any sons we produce together as only a mother can. You can choose to learn from her teachings, or..."

His son barely seemed to breathe. "Or?"

It was time to make himself clear. "You will attend to the formalities of this marriage and play the part of my dutiful heir and a gracious young lord, or you can attempt to win your way back into my good graces from exile at our winter home in Volcalen."

Zaden opened his mouth to protest.

"On one quarter your usual stipend. After all, if you are not my heir, you would not enjoy an heir's stipend."

"You cannot do that," his son growled.

"I can and I will. If you ever dare touch Rostana in anger again — touch her in any way but the most mannered — I will cut it in half again."

Zaden's hand closed into a fist.

"You have three choices, Zaden."

"And those are?"

"You know two of them," Gabel counseled.

Zaden offered a single tense nod of his head in agreement.

"Your final choice is admitting you are not man enough to celebrate the joyous additions to our family. If that is the case, you may retire to the estate in Volcalen, with your full stipend. At any time, you may choose to return to your duties here. If you choose not to return in a reasonable period of time, you forfeit your place as heir."

There was a moment of potent silence. "What do you consider a reasonable period of time?"

Gabel considered that. "Six years."

"Why six?" There was a note of suspicion in that.

"I imagine Rostana and I will produce a child within the year. If that child — male or female — has not seen you as a productive member of this household within the first five years of life, you forfeit your chance to do so."

Zaden hesitated and then nodded solemnly.

"But, Zaden..."

His son stared at him, abruptly wary. "Yes, Father?"

"If you choose to stay and you fault at the rules I have set for you — If you make miserable the celebration — If you make Rostana miserable in any way, there will be no forgiveness. There will be no winning your way back into my good graces. I will disown you tonight...or tomorrow or next week or next month."

Zaden swallowed hard, his face pale. His hand loosened.

"Do you understand me, Zaden?"

"I do. Quite clearly, Father."

"Very well. You have until dinner to make your decision." Gabel left without giving Zaden a chance to answer. *Any answer given in haste has not been considered well enough.*

* * * *

"Lady Renald?"

She looked up at Gabel's driver, blinking her eyes in exhaustion.

The driver offered his hand. He didn't press Rostana to take it. That would be presumptuous, as it would have been presumptuous to use her given name before she was lady of his manor. The hand remained, awaiting her leisure to accept his aid in stepping down from the coach or to dismiss the same.

Rostana took it for show, balancing herself out of the coach. He didn't presume to see her to the door. Before her father's house steward had opened the door for her, the driver had retaken his seat.

But he didn't pull away. "One hour before dinner bell, Lady Renald," he called out. "I will come for you then."

She looked over her shoulder and nodded her understanding. That accomplished, Rostana climbed the front stairs and slipped past Jos.

Her move to flee to her rooms ended halfway across the foyer when her mother folded Rostana into her arms. Her older sister came running, and several aunts followed. A trusted clothier sauntered from the library in their wake.

Rostana's cheeks heated in understanding. They knew. Gabel — or perhaps her father — had told them the tale already. She'd slept for hours, and Gabel had been dressed for town when she'd woken. He could well have left his manor for hours, and she would not have been the wiser.

"Oh, Rostana." Her mother's voice held not a hint of censure. If Rostana had to guess, she'd call the tone wistful.

She nodded, at a loss to answer a comment she didn't fully understand.

"Lady Renald?" the clothier prompted Rostana's mother. "We have little time, my lady."

Her mother pulled away and took Rostana by the arm. She led the way up the stairs and into her personal lounge, a large room attached to her mother's bedroom that was most commonly used for entertaining female guests of the lady of the manor.

Rostana had rarely entered the room. Now she found herself the center of attention in it.

Her sister and aunts settled on chairs and couches around the room, and the whirlwind began. The clothier stripped away Rostana's cloak, and her mother stopped and stared.

Rostana pressed a hand to her stomach through the borrowed dress. There was no question what concerned her. "My dress was rumpled. Gabel felt —" Her face burned at the intimacy of using her betrothed's given name in company. "H-he felt a clean, well-kept gown was a better choice than being seen in public in —"

"Of course it is." Her mother executed a theatrical turn, ever the gracious lady of the manor. "Now... Your ceremony. Red is the most common color, but you need not choose it, if it is not to your liking."

The implication was clear. Everyone expected Rostana to choose it, considering the circumstances leading to their speedy nuptials. Red was the color of Magmon and implied the heat of passion.

As such, it was the color Magmon's priests wore. Unbidden, Kar's face taunted her. She wasn't Kar's woman; she was Gabel's woman. "No. Not red."

The clothier tipped her head in acknowledgement, though it would make her job all the harder. "Have you a preference, Lady Rostana?"

I am Gabel's woman. The color must reflect that fact. Gabel's eyes were deep blue. *His impassioned eyes.*

"Lady —"

"Blue. Azulite blue, to be precise." She looked around, anticipating their displeasure at such an atypical choice.

The clothier smiled. "It will be most memorable." She motioned to a servant girl, who was already busy recording the information on two separate books.

One is for Gabel's servants. Though he would not be privy to all her choices, food and color choices were essential, since his household would be responsible for much of the decoration and cooking.

The clothier continued. "Your proving dress must be crystal white, but I can add accents of Azulite. Perhaps in your hair and at the train of your gown."

"That would be lovely." The full import of what she'd said hit Rostana solidly, and her stomach started to squirm. "Gabel requested a proving?"

Her mother's brow furrowed. "The king insisted on it, Rostana. It is required by law in cases where a resolution is requested and the bride is very young."

"Of course." Then Gabel hadn't asked for the display of willingness. That was relief.

Her sister appeared at Rostana's side and took her hand. "You are only required one woman of your family, one of Lord Tiben's, and one with no vested interest in the outcome."

Rostana squeezed her hand. "Would you, Rana?"

She smiled. "I am honored you asked me. I assume Lord Tiben will choose his female relative?"

"I would assume he will." Since Rostana didn't know the ladies, he would have to; she could hardly choose for herself.

"And your third?"

Rostana considered that. By law, it was supposed to be a married woman, and none of Rostana's contemporaries were married.

"Lady Amil?" her mother suggested.

Rostana bit back a wince. Missa Amil would hardly have been her first choice for a third. The woman was a friend of her mother's and her aunts', but she was also a jaded woman. Rumor had it that both Missa and her husband engaged in outrageous affairs, whether wintering in Frilan's Notch or summering in Aidalyn.

She opened her mouth to suggest another, sighed, and nodded her agreement. No matter who her mother suggested, Rostana was likely to find a reason to protest it. Nothing about this situation was perfect, least of all having one of her mother's contemporaries watching her having sex with Gabel.

"Very well. I will contact Missa. In the meantime, we must finalize the menu. Our cooks will prepare the baked goods. Lord Tiben's will prepare the rest."

The clothier stepped forward. "While you decide, I will take my measurements. The sooner I depart, the sooner I can design a wardrobe that will make brides to be envious for years."

Rana patted Rostana's hand. "And I will pack for you."

"Pack?" Rostana's head spun at the speed of events. It seemed too much was happening at once.

"Since you will be sharing Lord Tiben's bed, you will have need of clothing, jewelry, shoes... Borrowing one dress can easily be dismissed. Doing so on a daily basis would make you look the pauper."

Which would reflect badly on my father and my house.

I will be sharing Gabel's bed every night, though we are not yet wed. She nodded and whispered her agreement, stunned that such a thing was considered acceptable.

CHAPTER FOUR

Rostana stared at the carpet laid out for her, wondering at the expense Gabel was going to. The first night, the carpet had been Azulite blue. Tonight's version was crystal white, in deference to the proving.

The meal the evening before had been nerve wracking. Gabel's relatives within the city had flocked to greet the lord's surprise young bride. Though none of them had openly challenged her and even Zaden had been gracious, there had been tension in the air from the moment she'd descended the stairs from Gabel's rooms until they'd seen the last guest to the door and retired to Gabel's bed.

They hadn't discussed the proving, save Gabel's introduction of Lady Eldae Zuri, his aging aunt and the woman he'd chosen from his own family to witness the proving. Though the woman had been kind, there had been something calculating in her eyes.

"Rostana?"

Rana's voice sent her into motion, and she took the driver's hand. Once she was safely on the carpet, he turned back to assist Rana.

Her sister stared up at the manor. It was bedecked in banners of crystal white and Azulite blue, bracketed by banners with Gabel's family crest emblazoned on them.

"By the Fire God," Rana breathed. "I have never seen such a display. The man means to announce the event to all of Aidalyn."

Rostana took her arm, suddenly feeling small and frail. Together, they made their way inside.

The crowd was smaller than the one the night before. Lady Eldae Zuri was accompanied by her son. Lord Amil had accompanied his wife, though Rostana noted he made a blatant visual assessment of herself and Rana when they entered.

Rostana's parents were there, of course. If the proving went against Gabel, they would transport both Rostana and Rana home. If it didn't, Rana would still accompany them.

Zaden stepped toward her. He raised Rostana's hand and kissed the back, playing the part of the perfect young gentleman. "Welcome home, stepmother."

Before she could protest the irreverent form of address, Gabel did. "*Lady* Rostana will suffice." There was a warning couched in it.

"Of course, Father. As you wish." But his eyes made a mockery of his placating tone.

Rostana stiffened, drawing her hand from his embrace. Zaden bowed smartly and withdrew. To her surprise, Gabel didn't take his place.

Her father cleared his throat. "Have you been *educated* in what the proving entails, Rostana?"

"You dare?" Lady Eldae huffed.

Gabel was more restrained. He shot a bland look at Rojer.

"You know I must ask it," her father defended himself.

"Indeed, he must."

Rostana startled at the strange voice coming from behind her. She turned to face the speaker, and her mouth went dry.

King Aratten sat in the far corner of the room, hidden from her as she'd entered the library. He sipped his drink, what appeared to be Gabel's best brandy, his expression unreadable.

Rostana hurried to curtsy, her face licking flames of embarrassment.

He didn't reply to that. "Well, child. Have you?"

She struggled to find the words to reply. "No, Majesty. I know only that it is a sexual proving but not one of virgin's blood. And I know there will be three witnesses to the proving."

"Four," he corrected.

Rostana sought out Rana's face, confused and seeking an explanation for the misinformation she'd been given.

The king forged on, explaining for himself. "I will be behind a screen for your comfort, but I must witness."

She nodded faintly. "Yes, Majesty." *I have had an audience before, and the King will not be watching. I can do this. To marry Gabel, I* must *do this.*

He sipped the brandy. "The proving is a simple matter. The claim is that Lord Tiben affects you sexually."

He does. Saying it aloud wouldn't matter. This farce would continue, either way.

"Lord Tiben may not instruct you. He may not speak to you, save vocalizations in the heat of Magmon's fire."

Rostana nodded. It was to make certain Gabel wasn't using his age and experience to control her somehow.

"Aside from kissing you, Lord Tiben may not initiate any touch. You, however, may touch to your heart's content.

"Neither of you may remove clothing."

Her brow furrowed in confusion. "Then how will we consummate the proving?"

A wry smile pulled up at the king's mouth. "You will ask the ladies to undo the panel and Lord Tiben's trousers, but do not do so until Magmon's hunger sears you."

"Majesty?" What did that mean?

"The ladies will evaluate your readiness and that of Lord Tiben. They will determine your affectation in the moment."

She swallowed hard at what he might mean.

"Do you wish to marry Lord Tiben?" It was asked gently, more an encouragement than a challenge.

"Yes. Yes, I do."

He smiled broadly and pushed to his feet. "Then trust that Magmon will fill you with the fire to prove your need."

* * * *

Gabel clasped his hands behind his back, mindful of the rules of the proving. Still, the sight of Rostana in the ceremonial dress had him aching to touch her. In many ways, the proving would be harder on him than it would be on Rostana. It might be easier if his hands were tied down for it.

Rostana looked down the master's hall, then met his gaze as they turned down the guest hall and away from the bedrooms. He didn't reply to her silent query; if he dared instruct her, the proving was over and the resolution denied.

She rushed to rejoin the moving mass of people traipsing toward the far end of the manor. Though only the witnesses and principles had mounted the stairs, it was still a formidable number of people for so intimate an endeavor.

Her voice emerged, tentative. "Should we not retire to a bed?"

The king answered. "If you seek Magmon's fire, a few prayers would not go amiss."

Gabel rolled his eyes at that. Why couldn't the man simply tell her they would sample Magmon's hunger on the Dragon God's altar?

Rostana stopped short in the doorway to the prayer chamber, a gasp escaping her lips. Gabel grimaced. Considering her training at the temple in Magmalen, the Dragon God only knew what associations she might make to what was expected of her.

Rostana's sister and his aunt drew her toward the altar. Lady Amil leaned close to her to whisper instructions. Rostana nodded, turned her back to the altar, and placed her hands on the edge. Her cheeks were crimson in what was surely embarrassment, but her expression said she wasn't shying from the proving.

The king paused only a moment to watch her reaction. He took a taste of the fresh glass of brandy Lir had poured before they ascended the stairs, made his way behind the dressing screen that had been set up for him, and settled his old bones in a chair he'd brought to the manor himself.

The other witnesses spread out, taking their places to watch and listen for breaches of the rules. Rostana looked from one person to the next, and her gaze settled on Gabel.

Her skittishness melted away. Gabel swore he could feel her heat from halfway across the room. He marched toward her, his cock rising fast.

Rostana didn't meet him halfway. Her hands fisted on the edge of the altar, and her head tipped back, parting slightly for his kiss.

Gabel took full advantage of the invitation. His hands came up automatically. He stopped them a hand's-width from her face, fisted them, and forced them down. Pressing them to the top of the altar gave him focus toward controlling the urge to touch her.

Gabel kept his body away from hers so it couldn't be accused that he was convincing her by touch. It was maddening to have to taste her hunger and not act on it.

The kiss started out slow and deep, but in moments, it was something more, something nameless and scorching. Heat radiated off of her; hotter than the midday sun in Volcalen, it made Gabel want to strip naked.

Not allowed. He bit back a growl of frustration.

Rostana pulled away from the kiss. At first, he thought she was shying.

"Please, Gabel," she whispered.

He ground his teeth. He couldn't answer. He couldn't remind her what the rules were or how the proving had to progress.

Her eyes pleaded with him, and he willed her to remember the rules set for them both. Rostana looked down at one of her hands, fisted in the white silk altar cover set out for the proving. It unfurled, and Gabel's heart skipped in excitement.

Yes. Remember the rules.

Her hands cupped his waist and pulled. Gabel didn't fight her. Though the rules said he couldn't initiate touch, he could enjoy any touch she initiated. With his cock screaming for contact, the last thing he'd do was stop her.

Rostana moaned at the contact. Her hands moved up his abdomen and chest, tracing lines of muscle.

Gabel's hands fisted in the silk, and he brought his mouth down on hers again. She met him avidly, stroking her body against his.

It was torture. Her breasts came to hard points against his chest, and her scent made his head spin. Sweat plastered his shirt to his body. Too late, he considered that he should have removed his dinner jacket before the proving.

Rostana pulled at his shirt, and Gabel opened his eyes in shock. She couldn't do this, and he couldn't counsel her not to.

"Rostana, the rules."

Thank the Dragon God that her sister is allowed to and is willing to issue the reminder I can't.

Rostana's hands went still, and a rumble of complaint escaped her lips.

Gabel owed the elder Renald daughter his thanks. *When it won't cost us the resolution to marry.*

Eldae's sniff of disdain spoke her disagreement. Gabel made a note of it. If the woman dared lie about the proving, she would be banished from his sight forever.

Rostana dragged her mouth from his. "The clothing," she grumbled. "Rana, please."

Gabel took a step back, his heart thundering. Rostana's sister went to her knees and started undoing the fasteners at the front panel of the dress.

Lady Amil handled his trousers, then Gabel's cock. He straightened at the glide of her fingers. Though he'd never been subjected to a proving before, Gabel felt certain a hand job wasn't part of the examination.

"He is most ready," Amil stated loudly enough that the king would hear it. The rest was delivered in a whisper meant for Gabel's ears alone. "Moreso than most men your age would be."

He would have liked to protest her blatant offer, especially delivered in sight of his bride, but silence was part of the proving. Keeping his gaze locked on Rostana was better than glaring at *Lady* Missa Amil. The former would keep him ready for his bride, and the proving was all that mattered. *At least for tonight.*

Staying erect was important for more than the examination. If Amil knew how repulsive he found her, it would offend her, and she'd yet to report on Rostana's readiness.

"Of course my nephew is erect," Eldae offered in a haughty tone. "A Tiben is nothing if not honorable, cultured, and virile."

"So I see," Amil purred.

Rana looked up from the line of tiny hooks, gasping at the sight of Amil fondling him. "I dare say the man is erect and ready."

Amil pulled her hand away with an exaggerated sigh.

Gabel didn't echo it; he was too busy watching the frilled pantaloons appear in the slit of the dress. He moistened his lips, anticipating the many delights of the dress's design.

The garment was deliciously misleading; he knew the pantaloons were crotchless. It was an old design, intended to allow the male entry while hiding the female's body from the witnesses. It was an exciting mix of innocence and decadence, much like Rostana was herself.

Rana pulled the panel open fully, and Rostana's breathing hitched. Her sister stood, hesitated, then reached between Rostana's thighs. "By Magmon, she is so ready?"

Amil brushed Rana's hand away and stroked her fingers through the slit in the bloomers, prompting a hiss from Rostana. Gabel tensed at that. Had Amil used her fingernails against Rostana in an effort to kill her arousal?

"A little too ready, I think," Amil opined. "Perhaps a test for aphrodisiacs would reveal something of interest in this case."

Gabel ground his teeth at the accusation, seething in anger. Was she saying this because of some perceived slight? Or had Rostana's mother asked Amil to report unfavorably?

"Such a test is routine," Eldae snapped. "Tiben has no need of such petty fakery."

Gabel smiled. Whatever Amil's aim was, there was no question Eldae would side against her now. Short of Gabel or Rostana breaking the rules set for them,

Eldae would let nothing stand in the way of the resolution. The family's honor had been attacked, and no dowager worth her salt would stand for that.

"Move aside," his aunt commanded.

Amil complied, and Eldae took her place at Rostana's side. She reached between the younger woman's thighs, and Rostana dropped her head back with a groan.

"Filled with Magmon's fire and besieged by His hunger," Eldae decreed. "Nothing more."

Amil tipped her head in a show of her polite disagreement.

"Gabel, please," Rostana pleaded.

"A moment, child." Eldae's voice took on a soothing tone. "Spread your legs and welcome your husband in."

Rostana did so, and Gabel's cock jerked in anticipation of what was to come. Rana reached down and pulled back the fabric from one side of her slit. Eldae did the same on the other side, making certain Gabel had an unobstructed entry to her body.

A moment too late to steel himself for it, Gabel realized Amil had positioned herself to guide him into Rostana's body. Her hand was rougher this time. Gabel didn't make a noise of complaint about it.

He bent his knees and moved toward Rostana. Gabel sucked in his breath at the first glorious stroke of the cockhead against her heated slit. Her fluids wept down his crown and Rostana moved restlessly against him, little gasps escaping her lips.

Her head came forward, and she lowered herself onto him. All three witnesses moved away, just in time for Gabel to thrust into her. The motion forced her upward and onto the top of the waist-high altar.

Rostana caught herself with one hand, the other still fisted in his shirt.

Their joint cry echoed off the stark, stone walls. Rostana levered herself up and down minutely, whispering out pleas for more.

Gabel started thrusting, his mind muddled in indescribable pleasure. He cursed the rules aloud. If he had use of his hands, he could control the movement more effectively, take her faster and deeper, and increase both their pleasure.

Her legs came up and encircled his hips, the split skirt hanging loosely down the front of the altar. Visions of her doing this with nothing beneath the skirt shot his movements from fierce thrusts to mindless need unleashed on his bride.

"Hold me," she begged.

Gabel cursed fluently. Every instinct screamed for him to do just that, but the proving depended on strict adherence to the rules. He cursed again, his hips speeding in frustration. Her rising sounds matched his.

"Touch her," the king urged him.

His voice was close, from just beside Gabel somewhere. In that position, the king was watching every thrust.

It should have shamed Gabel that he didn't care, but the audience didn't matter. What was a man watching when three women already were?

He is a man...and powerful! What if he wants Rostana for himself? Gabel shook that thought away. It didn't matter if he was the king and already had a wife of his own. Gabel would fight any man, commoner or king, that had designs on Rostana.

"Touch her. The resolution is yours, Tiben. She lives for your cock, and I will counter any witness that says otherwise."

There was a warning couched in that, and Gabel didn't question he'd aimed it at Amil.

Gabel brought his hands down to her hips with a roar. The addition of his hands allowed him to position Rostana for hard, deep thrusts. With his support, she brought the hand from behind her and pulled at him.

Rostana climaxed screaming his name, and Gabel pounded hard into her contracting sheath. Her crest was waning when he gave in to the urge to release into her. That set off a second climax for Rostana, and she let out a piercing scream of pleasure.

They parted a bit in the aftermath, her body wrapped around his, both mussed and sweat soaked. As his mind cleared, their positions resonated with Gabel.

He was above her. At some indeterminate moment in their frenzy, he'd followed Rostana onto the altar. She lay with her head over the edge, her loose hair streaming toward the floor.

Her hands tightened in his shirt, and she pulled herself up by the grip, nestling her lips to his throat.

"Gabel."

Her whisper sent a shock down his spine, and his cock bucked within her. The urge to celebrate again on the altar was strong, but there were formalities to be met.

"Soon," he assured her.

"I will make your apologies, Tiben," the king offered.

"No. I will see to my duties." He smiled down at Rostana. "Quickly, I promise."

"As you wish," he conceded.

Gabel slid free of her body, sweeping the panels around her before any of the witnesses could see much of her. Her grip loosened, and he knelt up between her thighs. Gabel fastened his trousers, groaning at Rostana's look of longing.

"Tiben —" the king began.

"As quickly as I can." The vow was for Rostana, not for the king.

She nodded her agreement.

Gabel hopped down to the floor, feeling decades younger than he was. He lifted Rostana into his arms and turned for the doorway to the corridor. "You will wait in our bed," he informed her.

Rostana nibbled at his earlobe. "Do not be long."

His cock complained the wait. "I will not. How could I with such a beautiful and delicious woman waiting for me?"

There was no reply to that.

The king and the ladies waited for him at the top of the stairs. Gabel made short work of settling Rostana on the bed and returning to them.

King Aratten took the lead, Gabel at his heels, and the three ladies in the rear of the procession. Heads turned as they made their way down the stairs, and Lord Amil made a show of checking the time, his brow going up. It was a subtle non-comment on Gabel's quick end; there was little doubt of that.

Gabel stood with his hands clasped behind his back, well aware of how mussed he was. As if in response to it, Zaden took a hearty drink, his lip curling in what he would deny was disgust, Gabel was sure.

"The determination?" Rojer asked formally.

Rana spoke first. "Fire in the blood. He does affect her."

Eldae tapped her cane on the floor for attention. "A most virile man. The girl could not help but to be affected by his potency."

Gabel smiled, and Zaden took another drink.

Missa Amil paused so long, Gabel felt beads of sweat form between his shoulders. If she spoke against him, Aratten would have to stop him from killing the beast.

"Sufficient to prove the claims," she offered coolly.

It was clearly the least agreement she could offer and not appear overly moved by what she'd seen. Gabel forced his jaw to loosen and motioned to her behind his back, knowing Lir would see it. His house steward would be sure *Lady* Amil and her disgusting husband were removed at the earliest possible moment.

Aratten raised his glass and tipped his head to Gabel. "The resolution is yours. You may proceed with your plans at your earliest convenience."

Gabel smiled. He fully intended to, but there was one more thing to do before he retired to his bed and Rostana's body.

"My thanks to all who have offered of their time to witness and all who have joined us this joyous night. Please, take a moment to enjoy the hospitality of the house. I will take my leave."

Zaden drained his glass and turned toward the window, but true to their agreement, he didn't cause a scene or show rampant disrespect.

Gabel tipped his head to the room in general, shook the king's hand, and mounted the stairs, his heart pounding in anticipation. At the door, he called out Rostana's name. He stopped, the door handle fisted in his hand, his mouth going dry at the sight beyond.

She lay on the bed, the dress spread wide around her now-bare legs, her female curls peeking from the split. Gabel swung the door shut and savored the sight for a moment, unable to fathom what he'd done to find himself in such favor with the gods.

Rostana shifted one leg, seemingly unsure. "Is this right, Gabel? I have heard —"

She made it no farther. He crossed the room to her and captured her lips. Rostana pulled at his trousers, releasing his cock. In a heartbeat, he was inside her, venting cries of pleasure. It was over in minutes, and they lay together, hands trailing over clothing and under, discovering new delights.

Gabel licked his lips, already planning their next joining. He would bathe her and put the dress back on. Then he would savor every inch of her until Rostana begged for him again.

CHAPTER FIVE

Rostana shuffled the slips of paper on the dining table, searching for the one with baked goods on it. Planning her first holiday celebration was nerve wracking, but it was also exhilarating. She knew she could ask her mother for help — or Eldae — but there was something satisfying and intimate in planning it with only her own and Gabel's input.

Zaden sauntered into the room, and she pretended not to notice him. One could never count on Zaden's mood or manners. Until he proved himself in good spirits or ill, it was tempting fate to invite insult.

Rostana was well aware that Gabel would already have exiled his son from the house, had she complained to him about Zaden's behavior, and she was equally aware that Lir and the other servants had done so in her stead on more than one occasion. It was a faint and probably baseless hope of hers that Zaden would stop acting the spoiled child, and she would not be the wedge which came between father and son.

He stopped at his father's usual chair and plucked one of the lists from the table. Against her better judgment, Rostana looked up at him, stunned that he would be so bold.

Zaden's expression went from sadness to anger and back again several times, piquing her interest.

"Is there something amiss, Zaden?" she chanced asking.

His jaw tightened, and his eyes narrowed. "Perhaps I should spend the winter holiday in Volcalen." He dropped the paper on the table and turned to leave.

"But holidays are family events," she protested.

His glare made it clear he wanted to vent something horrible in response but dared not.

It was time to take her headstrong stepson by the ear and make herself clear, it seemed. "You are part of this family, Zaden, though you don't appear to see it that way. Your father loves you, though you frustrate him to distraction."

"And you, *Lady* Rostana? What do you feel? What do you want?"

Lir stuck his head out of the kitchen, and Rostana waved him away. The door closed, but she was certain he tarried nearby, listening for anything that might require his intervention or a report to Gabel.

"I want peace in our home. I want you to feel that this is still your home and your family, no matter the additions to it. And yes, I would like you to not think ill of me, as I try not to think ill of you."

"You wish me to feel that this is my home and my family." A snort followed.

"Of course. I never intended otherwise."

He motioned to the paper he'd tossed back on the table. "While you ignore family traditions I know and love? A fine way to show respect for me and *my* family."

Rostana picked up the paper and scanned its contents. It was food for the servants to pass in the hours before dinner. "I do not understand, Zaden. Your father never mentioned traditional foods that I should include when I asked. What would you —"

"Then he has replaced my mother with you, and I assume will replace me with whatever children you give him."

That stung. Rostana took a moment to calm her rioting heart. "There was a dish your mother added to the menu long ago that I am unaware of?"

His scowl answered that.

"If it means so much to you, add it. Please." She offered him the list and pen.

Zaden hesitated, and his expression changed to one of confusion. "You mean that? Sincerely?"

"Yes. I do. I never meant to exclude you from the plans. You just...never showed an interest in giving your opinion on the matter."

He reached out, and took the paper and pen gently from her hand. It took only a moment for him to scrawl something at the bottom of the sheet. Zaden hesitated a moment and then added a second item. Then he offered it back to her.

Rostana took it and read the additions. One was a smoked fish on bread, and the second was a type of cookie she had heard of but never tasted. "Thank you, Zaden. I will enjoy trying these, I am sure."

He nodded and turned again to go.

It is a waste to let him leave while we are gaining an understanding between us. "Zaden?"

He turned to look at her, his expression and stance wary.

"Are there any other traditions I should be aware of? Tiben's manor should not disappoint family or guest."

He seemed to consider that. After a moment, he returned to the table and took the seat across from her. "May I see the list of decorations?" he requested.

Rostana shuffled through the papers again, and handed it over with a smile. Perhaps there was a chance for Zaden yet.

* * * *

Rostana plucked another of the zorba fish cakes off the fresh tray from the oven and sampled it. Whatever Eldae's cook had done was sublime, and it seemed she couldn't get enough of the little treats.

Though the cook was surely exasperated with her, the kindly woman smiled and nodded her encouragement. That was all it took for Rostana to snatch up another. And another.

By the Dragon God, I will have no stomach for the meal if I continue this way. She ate still another, then asked for a glass of milk to wash them down.

She'd come to the kitchen to ask how preparations were proceeding, and before she knew it, she'd found herself held hostage to the damned little cakes.

"Rostana?"

She looked up, her mouth full of yet another zorba fish cake, and her cheeks went hot in embarrassment. Gabel was watching her, perplexed by her behavior, no doubt. Rostana swallowed and took a drink of the milk.

His brow furrowed again. "Are those zorba fish?"

"I'm afraid so. I am not sure there will be many left for the guests, at this rate," she admitted.

Eldae's cook chuckled. "I have trays and trays more, Lady Rostana."

Her stomach took notice, and Rostana groaned. "I may gain several stone from eating them."

"I thought you didn't like zorba fish." Gabel recalled that accurately.

Which left her at a loss to explain it. "I thought I didn't. Whatever this cook has done is nothing short of miraculous. I cannot seem to get enough of these little cakes."

Gabel shot a questioning look at the cook, and she shook her head in return. He crossed the room to Rostana and plucked a cake off the tray. His brow furrowed at the taste.

"Zorba fish," he confirmed. His look at Rostana was calculating.

She ran an unsteady hand down her robe. Wondering what he was thinking had her nerves on edge.

Gabel plucked the tray from the work table and offered her his arm. "Join me?" he invited.

Rostana wound her arm through his.

"Do not forget your milk," he reminded her.

One of the other servants rushed to refill it, then handed it to Rostana.

He ushered her to their bedroom and set the tray on the table beside the bed, motioning her to it. Her mouth watering, Rostana took him up on the offer and popped another of the cakes in her mouth.

"It occurs to me that your sudden change in likes and dislikes might mean something, Rostana."

That was enough to cause her to cough on the half-swallowed zorba fish cake. She took a drink of the milk and cleared her throat. "In what way?"

He paced the length of the room and returned. "This is not the first time you have had an uncontrollable urge for a certain kind of food. There were the powdered cookies just yesterday."

"A favorite of mine," she confessed.

"And the roast tubers earlier this week?"

Her face heated. She hadn't eaten anything else offered that night. *Just the tubers. Three servings of them.* There was no explanation for it but that they'd tasted so *right* to her. *Just as the zorba fish does.*

"But you've barely touched wine in days," he continued.

Rostana nodded. She'd already told him she believed a few of the bottles from that cask had soured somehow, and he'd countered the wine had tasted fine to him.

"Your stomach has been changeable in general of late."

"The excitement and stress of our first holiday party," she dismissed his concern. "I am certain nothing ails me."

"*Are* you certain?"

What was he implying?

Gabel crossed the room and settled on the bed next to her. Just as Rostana was about to ask what he meant, he brought one hand up and kneaded at her breast. His touch was potent, and she gasped in response.

His smile said her reaction told him something of importance.

"Gabel? What is it?"

"I believe I need to give Lir additional instructions."

"You do?" Nothing he was saying made any sense.

"I have been married before, Rostana."

"I know that." Why was he stating the obvious?

Gabel unfastened her robe and pulled the sides apart to bare her to the waist. Before she could form another question, he was tonguing one nipple, then the other.

Rostana fisted her hand in the back of his hair, her body wetting for more. *We have no time for this.* "Gabel. The guests will be arriving soon." It would be poor form not to be there to greet them.

He didn't reply to that. Instead, Gabel paid painstaking attention to her bare breasts. Her stomach quivered in appreciation, and her nectar heated and flowed for him.

I don't care how rude our late greeting appears. Rostana arched her back, forcing her nipple further into the heat of his mouth.

Gabel's hands retreated from her back, and he yanked his robe off. Then he parted hers and lifted her by the waist.

Rostana spread her legs, straddling him as he lowered her over his engorged cock. She started to lever herself up to ride him, but Gabel held her still, his cock filling her and stretching her.

"Gabel, please," she begged. His stillness was a torture.

He didn't reply; rather he pushed back at her shoulders, forcing them to the mattress to bring her chest up to a more comfortable position for his continued attentions. His suckling and licking at her chest became more avid.

Her channel started to flutter a warning that climax wasn't far off. "Oh. Oh, Gabel. I must. Please."

He suckled hard at a nipple, and she panted, whimpering at the difficulty of trying to stop her rise to release.

"I do not want to come without you."

He suckled hard at the other as if stating making her come without him — and so simply — was his intent.

His cock bucked against her inner walls. That spelled her end. Rostana released with a sob of indescribable pleasure.

As if the response spurred him on, Gabel suckled harder, moving from one breast to the other like a starving man faced with a feast. He left little bruises, then licked at them. The pleasure-pain forced her over again. Then again, in a tapestry of moans and scents, a sensual haze she'd never dreamed of.

At last, Gabel erupted into her. Rostana shouted his name, her throat aching.

Gabel released her breast and straightened, his body pressed tight to hers. His breath warmed her forehead, and she sank into his embrace, exhausted.

How much time had they spent locked in Magmon's hunger? Did she really care? Rostana conceded that she didn't.

When Gabel started to wane, he lifted her onto the mattress and pulled a blanket over her.

Rostana started to push it away. "The guests —"

Gabel shushed her and lifted the blanket over her again. "We have plenty of time. I need to speak to Lir for a moment. After that, we will bathe and dress."

She nodded wearily and yawned. Her eyes were closed before he had his robe tied shut around his body again.

* * * *

Gabel's heart skipped in excitement as he left Rostana napping and sought out Lir. The steward was in the kitchen, giving final instructions to the servants. Lir stopped mid-sentence at the sight of Gabel and waited for new orders.

An astute man. He always has been. "Continue," Gabel ordered. "But leave the final decorations for last. I have an addition to make."

If the order surprised Lir, he showed no sign of it. He tipped his head and went back to the minute details of favored allies, bearing or newly-delivered women they knew would be in attendance, and order of service. At last, he stopped and nodded to Gabel again.

"I will need to speak to you, Lir, as well as the cooks, one server, and three of the men who can be spared from other tasks."

There was a moment of stillness, and all the servants stared at him as if he'd spoken ancient Set.

"The others may leave," Gabel added crisply. "You all have work to attend to."

Lir pointed out four of the assembled servants and waved the rest away. They moved closer to Gabel, and the cooks left their preparations and gathered around as well.

Gabel bit back a smile at the nervous glances they shot each other. "My wife, the Lady Tiben, is bearing."

He'd suspected it when she had an almost imperceptible bleed at her last cycle. She was due for another any day, but every indication was that it would certainly not come. After the light cycle, coupled with her sensitivity to touch and foods and her exhaustion after such minor loveplay, there was no doubt left in his mind.

The server pressed a hand to her mouth and unsuccessfully stifled a squeal of delight. Her cheeks darkened and she mumbled an apology for interrupting him.

Gabel addressed her first. "You will serve my wife tonight. Accompany her, if she feels the need to mingle. Fetch whatever she asks for immediately. If you notice she shows a preference for anything in particular, bring her an ample supply."

She curtseyed and nodded emphatically.

He focused on Eldae's cook. "It seems your zorba fish cakes are momentarily a favorite of my child. Make certain there is plenty for any demands my young heir makes."

"Yes, Lord Tiben. Of course."

"Send servants to the marketplace for anything you think you might require." Gabel ranged his gaze down the line of cooks. "That includes all of you. I have no idea what my heir might decide to demand next. Check your stores of fresh meat, fruits and vegetables, spices... Whatever you are low on, order early in the day, and be prepared to cook whatever my wife might desire."

He focused on the bakers. "Make more of the powdered cookies. We already know my wife has a fondness for them."

The younger baker started to turn to do so, then planted her feet and waited to be sure Gabel was finished with his orders.

He searched out the eldest of the male servants Lir had ordered to stay. "Tilner, you were here when my first wife was bearing. Do you recall the setup she favored for entertaining?"

The older man seemed to consider it. "I believe so, Lord Tiben."

"Instruct the other two in the preparations, but since this will be announced as part of the celebration, a drape to hide them would be best. Take the nursing lounge from the nursery and quilts and pillows from the linen room, but be quiet about it. Rostana naps at the moment."

He nodded.

Gabel considered him for a moment. "Typically, I would ask Lir to escort Rostana in my absence, but Lir has duties to perform. You will be responsible for aiding Rostana, should she become dizzy or ill."

She was ill when she complained about the wine, he reminded himself. Has she been dizzy as well? Unbalanced? It was possible. Likely.

Tilner tipped his head. "I will be honored to, mi'lord."

"Very well. You all have work to do. Go to it." Gabel turned to leave.

"Lord Gabel?" Lir called out.

He stopped in surprise. "Yes, Lir?"

"Should I make your apologies to any early guests?"

Gabel chuckled. "Not at all, Lir."

"But they will assume —"

"I know very well what they will assume. They will be incorrect, will they not?" He raised an eyebrow at his steward and made his way back to Rostana's side.

As he'd expected, she was curled under the blanket, sleeping soundly. He let Rostana snooze while he prepared a bath for her and laid out her clothes. Then he brushed the backs of his fingertips along her cheek and called her name softly.

Rostana stretched and opened her eyes. Her smile for him faded as she glanced at the clock. She scampered to her feet and reached for her underclothes.

Gabel took her hand and brought it to his mouth for a kiss. "No worries, Rostana."

"The early guests will be arriving soon, Gabel."

"Family, and family will understand if we are a few—"

"Are you mad? This is our first holiday gathering." She reached for the clothing again, and he gathered her hands in his.

Gabel sighed. "Come. Our bath is waiting."

"We do not have time, Gabel."

He lifted her into his arms and carried her to the tub. Rostana didn't fight him as he placed her in it, though she was clearly agitated. Gabel joined her, sighing as she rushed through the process of bathing.

"Slowly," he soothed her.

Rostana looked up at him, her throat bobbing as if she was about to cry.

By the gods, I forgot how brittle a woman's emotions are when she is bearing. Every moment in Rostana's company confirmed what he knew to be true. "No one will rush you, Rostana. Not now. Not in the foreseeable future."

"I do not understand you," she complained. "This is our first holiday gathering. They will say I am a poor hostess and probably that you are thinking with your cock instead of your head."

It was hard not to laugh at her crass description. "We will be down there before any persons outside the family arrive. Family will forgive our tardiness when they hear our news."

Her brow creased in confusion, and she paused in scrubbing at her skin. "News? What news will they hear?"

Gabel smiled and moved to her side in the big tub. He placed a hand over her womb. "Bearing women are never rushed, Rostana. Bearing women sit when they need to. They eat what and when they will, and they sleep when their bodies call."

She stared at him, her mouth working at words that didn't emerge.

"You were napping. The staff had been ordered not to wake you. The reason for it will become clear when we make our announcement."

"So you intend to lie to them?" The horror in her tone was impossible to miss.

"I will not be lying, Rostana," he offered patiently.

"I have not even missed my blood flow," she protested.

"Near enough, and... I have been married before."

"I *know* that, Gabel. Why do you feel the need to remind me of it?"

"Because I know the signs of a bearing woman. I saw Korenna through them, and I would have to be blind to miss them in you."

She stared at him, open-mouthed. "The food likes? They are not acute, and —"

"I disagree, but they are also not the only signs."

Rostana placed a hand over her eyes and took several deep breaths.

"You are faint," Gabel guessed. How many times had he mistaken that move for frustration?

"Oh, stop, please," she begged him. There was no heat in it. Rostana leaned into his chest. Just when he was sure she was about to drop off to sleep again, she spoke. "How do we announce this news? I don't believe I've ever been in attendance when such an announcement was made."

Gabel smiled, envisioning just that.

* * * *

"Is this really necessary?" Rostana asked.

"After you felt faint, you ask if it is necessary for me to escort you down the stairs? Yes, Rostana. It is quite necessary, and you will have servants with you if I am not."

Bearing for less than an hour, and he is already intolerable. I never believed Mother's stories about men with bearing wives.

Two steps down — and her head still spinning lightly — Rostana was abruptly thankful for Gabel's arm around her waist. Not that she was about to admit it to him.

The guests below went silent and looked up at them expectantly. Zaden tried to hide a scowl behind his drink. That was enough to clear a bit of the batting out of Rostana's head.

Short-lived as it was. A moment later, the sensation of falling assaulted her and she grasped at

Gabel's hand. A dizzying moment later, she was in his arms.

So much for making an announcement.

"Tilder, if you would," Gabel ordered.

Rostana bit back a groan and squeezed her eyes shut to his movements. She settled on a lounge with pillows for her head. Gabel ordered someone to place more pillows under her feet, and a blanket covered her.

"Is she ill, Gabel?" Lady Eldae demanded. "By the gods, man, the child should be abed and not trying to host a party."

"I am not a child," Rostana grumbled. She forced her eyes open, then swallowed a sour lump at the sight of the sea of moving, festive colors.

Gabel sighed. "Not precisely how I wanted to make our announcement."

The colors stopped moving suddenly; it was a blessing for her abused senses.

"Announcement?" Zaden's voice added a chill to the room.

Gabel took her hand and kissed the back. "Rostana is bearing."

A cheer went up, and Rostana managed a smile that felt decidedly weak.

Zaden didn't cheer. For a moment, Rostana was certain he meant to leave the house and never return. Then he nodded to her and raised his glass in salute.

Though she had no clue what he meant by it, she nodded in return. Hopefully, it was a good sign and not a bad one.

CHAPTER SIX

Rostana moaned, shifting uncomfortably. She was exhausted, but she hadn't slept well in days. The babe kicked and rolled, waking her from even deep sleep, over and over again.

Perhaps milk will calm him and allow me to nap. She wasn't hungry. but that was hardly surprising with Gabel's son filling her belly near to bursting. Soups and milk seemed to be all she could stomach most days, and she knew it worried Gabel. He'd consulted the priestess healers more than once about the subject.

She rang the bell for Lir and waited. There was no answer. Rostana rousted herself from bed and pulled a robe around her sleeping gown. If no one could hear her ring, she would seek out one of the servants to aid her.

No one answered her call at the doorway to their bedroom, so Rostana made her way toward the stairs. She hesitated at the top. Gabel had requested she not attempt to navigate the stairs without help, but help didn't appear to be anywhere near. *For once. After months of the entire household hovering, now I cannot find a servant anywhere.*

Rostana looked down at the staircase, abruptly nervous. She couldn't even see her feet. It was no wonder Gabel worried about her navigating the stairs.

Oh, this is ridiculous. If I hold tight to the balustrade and keep my feet close to the ground, I will be fine. She made her way down the first dozen steps without incident.

The pain came without warning, and the Mother's waters gushed down her legs in the wake of it. Rostana sank to the stairs, gasping for breath, her hands and knees quaking.

Panic set in. She couldn't possibly walk on the wet marble stairs, especially not in her unsteady state, and lowering herself down them on her backside was no safer.

"Lir?"

No one came to her call.

Rostana bit back a sob of frustration and doubled around another pain. "Lir!"

Pounding feet closed on her position, but it wasn't Lir. Zaden rushed up the stairs with a series of curses his father would surely disapprove of.

"What are you doing?" he demanded. "You could be injured." His eyes widened, and he panned his gaze down her body and up again. "*Are* you injured?"

Rostana shook her head. "The babe," she gasped.

Zaden ran his fingertips through the pool of Mother's waters and rubbed his thumb against them, testing the slick. "Good gods! Why didn't you ring for Lir?"

"I *did.* No one answered my call." Tears pooled in her eyes.

He pushed to his feet, his face darkening in seeming frustration. "Servants!" Zaden bellowed.

One of the cooks emerged from the dining room, looking rattled. "Yes, mi'lord?"

"Fetch Lir. Send someone for my father and a second for a priestess healer. The servants have permission to use my horse and Rostana's. Whatever is needed to accomplish it all."

"Lord Zaden? Lady Rostana?"

Zaden lifted Rostana into his arms and shot a glare at the cook. "Move, woman! My father's young heir is on his way." He started to turn and then stopped. "And send a maid to clean these stairs before someone slips and kills herself."

Rostana was certain that last statement had been a subtle dig at her, but she was too exhausted to care.

The cook was out of sight before Zaden had moved two steps. At the far reaches of the house, voices rose in a cacophony of overlapping calls and shouts.

Zaden took Rostana back to bed, settled her on the mattress, and piled all the pillows at the headboard. He turned his back. "What do you need? A shift? A fresh sleeping gown?"

Rostana shook her head, then went still in the realization that he couldn't see it. "No. Why ruin a second?"

He waved his arm. "Cover yourself and let me know what else I can do to aid you."

Rostana removed the robe and pulled the blankets up, tucking them beneath her arms. "I am covered, Zaden." She had a hard time looking at him. That made little sense, considering she'd set out to seduce him when she returned from Magmalen.

He appeared at the bedside, looking harried. "What can I do for you?"

"You have already done it. My thanks for it." She meant it. He'd done everything she might have hoped for.

Zaden nodded grimly. He stared at her for a moment, then started pacing. At every wince or moan, Zaden snapped back, his arms tightening as if in expectation of a fight, his expression slightly manic.

A few tense moments later, a quick, hard knocking echoed through the room. Zaden waited for her nod before shouting out an order to enter.

Lir launched into the room, looking not at all himself. His clothing was mussed and his hair windblown. The steward took a moment to smooth his appearance, then bowed to her.

"Tilder is on his way to collect Lord Gabel, Lady Rostana. Nol is on his way to collect the healer priestess. What can I do for you?"

"Why does everyone ask that?" she complained. "Unless you know a way to deliver my son for me, there is *nothing* you can do." It was the pain speaking, and she hoped they would forgive her the ill treatment later.

The pain worsened, and Rostana panted, pressing back into the pillows, rubbing her distended womb with shaking hands. A sob escaped her, and Rostana bit a second back ruthlessly.

Zaden seemed to snap. "Lir. Bring warm water and bathing cloths. I have read that bathing the woman's head and face will help relax her during labor."

The steward nodded and rushed away to comply.

Rostana stared at Gabel's son, amazed by the order he'd given. "Where would you read such a thing?" It wasn't the sort of thing a man would have an interest in learning.

He shifted from foot to foot, looking for a moment more like a young boy than the fully-grown man she knew him to be. Zaden cleared his throat, his gaze traveling the far corners of the room.

"I thought it might be...useful to know about childbirth, considering you are carrying my younger brother into this life."

Another pain assaulted her, and Rostana gasped out a response. "Not for long, it seems."

Pains came and went. Lir brought the water, and Zaden went to work, bathing her head and face, making whispered promises that all would be well.

When the unmistakable feeling of the babe descending assaulted her, Rostana looked at her two caregivers, panicked. "Where is the priestess healer? There is little time left."

Lir ran his fingers through his hair, leaving spikes in his wake. "Soon. It must be soon."

Zaden hesitated, then started rolling his sleeves. "Tell the cooks to bring hot water and soap, Lir."

The steward shot him a look that said he found the command scandalous. "Lord Zaden, you have never delivered a babe before."

"Neither have you or anyone else within the household," he answered patiently. "At least I have read about it."

"Read about it?" Rostana gasped out. He was joking. Dragon's Fire, he had to be joking.

Zaden turned to her, his expression pained. "I am the closest thing to a healer we have, Rostana. Until she arrives, please allow me to do what I can."

She hesitated long enough to note the rising of another pain. "Yes. Anything. I do not want to do this alone."

Lir tipped his head and bolted for the stairs.

Zaden watched him go, then focused on her again. "I give you my solemn vow that I only mean to aid my brother into the world in any way I can. I mean you no harm. Nor him. Do you trust me, Rostana?"

Despite his deplorable actions and words early in her marriage to Gabel, Zaden had been nothing short of a gentleman since he'd helped her plan the holiday party. "Yes. I trust you."

He nodded. "I will do all I can."

* * * *

Gabel vaulted from the coach, his councilor's robes half off. Tilner sprinted to the front door ahead of him and opened it for Gabel with a tip of his head.

Inside, the household servants were gathered in the foyer, pacing aimlessly, as if there was no other work to be done. Gabel stared at them in shock.

"What in the Fire God's name is going on here?" he demanded.

Nol, the wine steward, looked up sharply. "Lady Rostana labors," he stated.

"I know it." Gabel pulled off the robes and handed them to a servant in laundry uniform. "Why are you all here and not doing your work?"

Nol looked around at the other servants. When no one answered in his stead, he cleared his throat and addressed Gabel again. "Lir ordered us to be ready for any orders he relays. All of us."

Gabel started across the foyer toward the stairs. "Has the priestess healer sent down many orders?" If she had, there might be a problem.

The silence made Gabel's heart pound. He turned to look at them, unnerved by the lack of reply.

The head cook answered that time. "There was no healer priestess available, Lord Gabel. They are all tending to...more acute cases. They have promised to come at their earliest convenience."

"Convenience? Smoke and fire! The babe will not wait for their convenience. What help does Rostana have?" A few of the female servants winced at his curses. All of them stared at him as if afraid to answer.

Rostana's shout sent Gabel up the stairs toward their room. Before he turned down the corridor, a babe's cry echoed. He would have liked to have claimed that put his mind at ease, but Zaden had cried as well. *Before his mother died on the birthing bed.*

Gabel burst through the door and into the room, stopping cold in surprise. Rostana reclined against a stack of pillows, Lir bathing her brow. Zaden stood at the foot of the bed, holding a bloodied, squalling infant.

His elder son looked up, smiling. "Mad as a wet songbird, but he's doing well, as far as I can tell."

Gabel was torn between going to Rostana and meeting his new son.

Zaden laughed. "Go to her. He will be waiting when you finish."

He nodded and went to Rostana's side, calling her name softly. His bride opened her eyes at the sound of his voice and offered him her hand. Gabel took it and sank to the mattress next to her.

Her skin was cool and her color light, but Rostana seemed to be in good health otherwise.

Not like Korenna. Thank the gods! It had been apparent that she was in distress within moments of their son's birth. She had been dead in less than an hour.

"Are you well?" he asked, relieved that she seemed in good spirits and not suffering ill effects, beyond what most women did.

Rostana nodded. "Thanks to Zaden and Lir."

Gabel shot a look of surprise at his elder son. "Zaden?" He'd thought Zaden had helped Lir deliver, but a closer inspection showed the house steward barely ruffled while Zaden's shirt was rolled to above the elbows and streaked in blood. "Zaden delivered you." He didn't question it.

"Thank the gods of fire and ice he was interested enough to read on the subject of childbirth when he learned I was bearing," Rostana praised him.

Zaden's face went a vibrant shade of red.

Gabel forced himself to speak. "Thank you, Zaden. Well done."

His son hesitated. He focused on the babe in his arms, and wrapped the clean towel around his younger brother. Zaden managed a tight smile and offered his wiggling bundle to Gabel. "I should go wash up." He clapped a hand on Lir's shoulder. "You should tell the servants to get back to work. The cooks, especially. Rostana will need a meal...red meat and milk, most of all."

Lir preceded Zaden out of the room. His son cast one last look back at the bed before closing the door.

Gabel stroked a finger over his son's hand, and the babe grasped it firmly. He chuckled. "He's going to be a strong one."

Rostana groaned. "Tell me about it. The child can kick like a horse."

"What are we going to name him, Rostana?" They'd discussed the possible names for months, but they'd never settled on a single one.

"Is it my choice now?" she teased. "You've been so opinionated on the subject, I thought for certain he would be dedicated before we chose one."

He raised an eyebrow. "You did do an incredible amount of work in bearing and birthing him," he conceded.

Rostana seemed to consider it. "Davril. I still like Davril."

"Davril it is."

* * * *

It wasn't a surprise to find Zaden waiting for him when he left their bedroom to see to a tray for Rostana. Gabel waved his son along, taking the stairs slowly to allow Zaden to speak his mind.

To his amazement, Gabel found he feared Zaden would choose to leave, to take time away to consider his options. Now that Davril had been born, Gabel wanted something this house had ever been denied. A proper family.

Zaden didn't hesitate. "You really did *want* this child." It wasn't a question.

"Yes." Why would Zaden question it?

"Why?"

Gabel stopped and stared at him. "Why what?"

"What made you want another child?"

"Rostana. A man in love wants a living representation of that love. It is Magmon's way."

Zaden stared at him. "It is more than that." Again, he didn't pose it as a question. He didn't wait for an answer either. "I saw you when you rushed into the room. You didn't know which to go to first."

Gabel nodded. "The love of a husband is very different than the love of a father, but neither is inherently more powerful than the other. One will never replace the other, and...in many ways, one feels incomplete without the other."

Silence fell between them.

"I suppose I do not explain it well," Gabel apologized.

"No. I think I understand it." He paused a moment. "Does my brother have a name yet?"

Gabel smiled widely. "Rostana has chosen the name. Davril."

Zaden seemed to consider it. "A strong name. It suits him."

Gabel waved the maid toward Rostana; she rushed from the dining room doorway with the tray of food and mounted the stairs at a near run. When she passed by them, Zaden started speaking again.

"I know you'd planned for me to follow you into the council chamber, but..."

"Go on."

He sighed. "I think I might like to learn surgery techniques instead. Davril can certainly train for politics."

Gabel considered it. He glanced up the stairs. "I think you might be good at that. A fine choice."

Zaden smiled, tipped his head, and headed down the stairs, looking more at ease than Gabel could remember seeing him in years.

CHAPTER SEVEN

"A missive from the royal house, Lord Tiben," Lir announced.

Gabel looked up from Davril and put out a hand for it. Rostana hurried to take their son, still spooked by the mention of the king, no doubt. He smiled his encouragement at her and broke the seal.

His joy fled at nearly the first word on the parchment. He cursed the timing.

No. Any timing would have been unwelcome, save perhaps her final weeks carrying. At that point, even the priestess healers would have forbidden travel, even as far as the palace, which was only two hand of hectar away.

"Gabel?" Rostana called. "Is something amiss?"

"No." He winced at the sharp edge to his voice.

Far from discouraging her, Rostana seemed to feel he needed comforting. Her hand closed on his knee. "Gabel?"

"It is nothing," he lied. *It is everything. Or it could be everything.*

"I am your wife. Am I not?" There was something meek and injured in the asking that made his heart ache.

"Of course you are," he soothed her.

"Then tell me what troubles you. Husbands do such things."

Gabel hesitated, unsure of how to reassure her.

"Or..." She paled a shade or two. "Perhaps you do not trust me."

"It is only an invitation I intend to send my regrets in response to." He hoped she'd be relieved at not having to face the king again.

"One does not refuse the king or the princes without good reason to do so."

She would know it. Her father was the king's man. Rostana's education would have included courtly manners. He needed a reason equally compelling.

"Davril is too young for such an affair, and he is too young to abandon the breast."

His fervent wish for her to agree with him died an unhappy death at her logical answer.

"We traveled as far for his dedication, Gabel, and nursing babes are always welcome at social events...save those tawdry little sexual parties *some* nobles throw." Her cheeks pinked at that comment. "I am certain the king would not invite a married man to such an event."

"Certainly not." Something told Gabel it would be wise to move Rostana to a new topic quickly.

She bested his time and returned to the original subject. "Then I fail to understand —"

"This is not a small gathering, Rostana. It will be — "

"The cen-centennial?" Her eyes sparkled in excitement Gabel cursed for the first time since he'd met her. Usually, her expressive eyes delighted him.

"Yes. So, you see —"

"Oh, Gabel! We must go. We simply must." She patted his knee, nearly squirming in place on the lounging couch she shared with him. Her eyes pleaded with him for his agreement.

"Rostana..." But what could he say to convince her?

The truth!

No. That wasn't an option.

"We must," she insisted. "We will be long dead before even a centennial comes again, and the Walking Gods offer blessings for babes in the crowd. Mothers are —"

"No!" His patience snapped at the mention of the He-Atal. "I will send our regrets, Rostana."

She stared at him, her expression stung and injured as he'd never seen her.

And I caused it. Damn me.

It is necessary. The truth will hurt her worse. How many times had he shuddered at the idea of Rostana learning how the He-Atal, *Lord* Karliss Furia, had played at her affections and her innocence.

Rostana rose without another word, Lir supporting her elbow to be sure of her balance while carrying Davril. She hurried from the library, Lir at her heels and offering to carry the babe for her.

Gabel let her go, praying he hadn't just destroyed his marriage.

* * * *

"You selfish, old bastard."

Gabel shot a look he was certain showed the depth of his shock and indignation at his elder son. "What did you say to me?"

Zaden stood there, his arms crossed over his chest. There was nothing of the petulant child of a year earlier in his stance or his tone. His expression spoke of the fire of his fury, and his tensed muscles of resolve as immovable as ice. "I am certain you heard it," he challenged Gabel.

"Would you care to explain it?" But he expected he knew.

"All this time, I've watched. I *thought* I was learning something of value from you and from Rostana, but it was all a sham. A politician's game."

Not what I believed he would say. "What was a game?"

"Did you ever love Rostana? Or was she simply a tool to use against me? A way to teach me a costly life lesson?"

"Did I — ? I assure you, Zaden, I *do* love Rostana. I have from nearly the first moment I saw her arguing with you in the tavern."

"You love her?"

Gabel nodded.

"And you do this?" Zaden motioned to the stairs, his expression hardening further. He didn't give Gabel time to reply.

"For the last year, I have endured daily rebuke, spoken and unspoken, on the subject of how I should have treated Rostana." He hesitated, seemingly pained. "What you did today has made a mockery of every lesson you have dealt me in a year."

"What precisely do you think I have done?" Surely, it bore no resemblance to the facts.

"You may be an old man, but —"

"I am not old." At fifty-seven, Gabel wasn't even middle-aged yet. *I still have a few years until I reach that milestone.*

"I am not finished," Zaden ground out from between clenched teeth.

Gabel motioned for him to continue.

"You may be an *older* man, but Rostana is an exceptionally young woman. The cen-centennial is *the* social event of a hundred lifetimes. Literally. A young woman would move the stars in the sky to acquire an invitation to such an event. She was offered one, and you refuse to let her attend."

"There is —"

"I am not finished, Father."

Gabel sighed. There was a decidedly infuriating side to his son becoming a responsible adult. "Continue."

"I intend to.

"She is also a doting mother to Davril. Mothers are central at the celebration of the Walking Gods. The babes are blessed by the gods. Rostana, like any young mother, considers it neglectful to deny Davril such a blessing, if she has the power to procure it."

There was a moment of tense silence between them.

"Are you finished?" Gabel asked archly.

"Not quite." Another moment of silence followed. "Your decree was callous and unfeeling. After all your warnings to me not to make Rostana miserable in her new home, *you* made her cry. How dare you treat her so shamefully."

There was little Gabel could say in response to that. He didn't doubt that Rostana had cried after she fled his presence. He sighed.

Zaden strode toward him, crossing his arms over his chest again, his expression grim. "What do you intend to do about it?"

Gabel took a calming breath. "There are facts you do not possess, Zaden."

"Then tell me."

The sorry tale refused to emerge. "I cannot, but trust that refusing to allow Rostana to attend is the only way I have to shield her from even more pain."

"Then tell *her* that."

"And cause her pain?"

"You are causing her pain now. I fully believe Rostana would prefer thinking of you as a doting husband intent on protecting her than one that disregards her feelings."

There was nothing in that logic Gabel could argue. "You are likely correct about that."

Zaden took a step back and motioned Gabel on his way.

A weak smile curved Gabel's lips. "One lesson remains you still need to learn, Zaden."

"And that is?" One brow went up that spoke his disbelief.

"One offers a wife a considered apology, not a rushed and haphazard one."

His son scowled at him. "Do not wait too long to offer it. A woman like Rostana is one of a kind. Given half a chance, I would right my own wrongs with her. At your expense, if necessary."

"Zaden!"

"Only if you fail to be a proper husband to her. If you do, you have no right to protest who is willing to be one."

* * * *

The tapping at the nursery door made Rostana's eyes sting with fresh tears. She didn't answer. Perhaps Gabel would think she was sleeping and leave her to another exhausting cry that might do the trick of providing such respite.

"Rostana, please. Let me enter."

He hadn't even tried the latch. Gabel thought she was the type of wife who would lock her husband away from her and from his own child?

Gabel tapped again. "Rostana?"

Her anger won out, though she kept her voice low to avoid waking Davril. "A woman does not lock a lord out of rooms in his own home," she informed him.

"May I enter?" There was something stiff and formal in that.

"It is your home. Go where you wish." Rostana wiped away fresh tears. It was *his* home. Strange how she'd never considered that before.

"It is our home, Rostana, and I will not impose myself on you. I beg an audience to explain what I did."

That shocked her to silence. Rostana hadn't expected Gabel to admit he'd done anything he should need to explain. Her father never would have.

"Rostana?"

"Come in."

The latch lifted and retracted, and Gabel pushed the door wide. For a moment, he stared at her, looking not at all the self-assured councilor she knew him to be. Inexplicably, she wanted to soothe him.

Outrageous. "Yes, Gabel?" Keeping her voice smooth and her lip from quivering took the last of her reserves.

"I apologize for my behavior. I never meant to hurt you or cause you to feel dismissed."

It was more than her father had ever offered, but it wasn't enough. "You said you had an explanation," she prompted him.

Gabel glanced at the open door. "Perhaps our bedroom would be a better —"

"Have I said I mean to stay there?" Her heart broke, even as she uttered the threat. How had their marriage come to this? And so quickly?

He paled. "No. You — you have not. Do you mean to move to the —?"

"I do not know what I mean to do," she admitted.

A sigh that sounded of relief escaped him. "May I explain?"

"I wish you would, if you can." Rostana winced. She sounded like an ill-mannered child, but she couldn't seem to help herself.

Gabel closed and latched the door. For a few heartbeats, he looked anywhere but at her directly.

Something in that unnerved Rostana, and her heart pounded in apprehension. "Gabel?"

He met her eyes, his earnest in resolve. "I do not want you to meet the He-Atal," he stated.

"Why?"

He didn't reply immediately.

"All He would do is bless Davril." What could be troubling about that?

"And lay hands on you as Davril's mother," he grumbled in return.

"A simple blessing." It wasn't as if the god had any intentions of more. Why would a god seek out another when he had his goddess? Rumor had it that the Walking Gods had committed in marriage.

"I do not want *Him* to touch you." His voice was rough, his hands in fists so tight his knuckles were lined in stark white.

"Are you unwell?" Gabel sounded crazed. What could unbalance him this way?

"I promised. I vowed not to allow it."

The moment of sacrilege their first morning together played out in her mind. "It was pillow talk, Gabel. I would never hold you to that vow."

"No. It was a promise to spill the young God's blood if he dared touch you." His expression said he wasn't exaggerating.

"I do not understand this," she admitted. "Why would you hate the Dragon God's Vessel so vehemently?"

He laughed harshly. "Jealousy. Fear that I would not be enough for you, if He —"

"You believe me a wanton," Rostana choked out.

"Never." Gabel sounded offended at the idea of it.

As was she. "You do. You think I would abandon you at the first touch of the —"

"He has touched you before, Rostana." It came out little more than a growl.

She shook her head, at a loss to account for that mad accusation. Had his mind snapped?

Gabel motioned for patience. He strode to her and sank to one knee. "I had hoped you would never have to know it. I feared His deception would...upset you."

"But, Gabel, I have never met the —"

"There are no priest concubines, Rostana."

She felt the blood draining from her face, and her breathing hitched at his pronouncement. "There has to be another explanation." It came out more a plea than a statement.

"The He-Atal was training in Magmalen when you were there."

Rostana opened her mouth to reply.

"At the temple."

A lump lodged in her throat, choking her lightly. "And the mark?" Gabel had asked if the priest had a mark.

He nodded solemnly. "It is the mark of the God's hand. It identifies the Dragon God's Vessel."

Her mind rejected it. "No. Kar — H-he cannot —"

"His name is Lord Karliss Furia," he offered in a soothing voice.

"A prince?" she squeaked. Rostana had bedded with a man that was both a prince and a God Vessel? She lay back on the lounge, abruptly faint. "Why did you never tell me?"

"They deceived you, Rostana. They had ample reason to do so, I assure you. No one but the priests, the royal family, the God Vessel's birth family, and a few trusted advisors to the king are permitted to know who the He-Atal is until just before the celebration of the Walking Gods."

"Then you didn't know who...?" Her hand moved in a shaking circle.

"Not until the day of Davril's dedication." He hesitated. "I am sorry, Rostana. I only meant to protect you. You were so innocent."

"Naïve, you mean. Dragon's smoke, how could I be so blind?"

"Young," he breathed. "Beautiful. So trusting and innocent. I loved you nearly on sight."

Tears stung at her eyes at his description of her. "You are truly jealous of the He-Atal?"

"Insanely." A wry smile pulled up at his lips.

"Why?"

Gabel didn't seem to know how to answer that.

Rostana pushed herself to sitting so she was eye to eye with him again. She cocked her head to one side and brushed a kiss against Gabel's mouth. "Why would you be jealous of Him? Kar has never had my love and never will. Unless you are jealous of his goddess —"

His growl nearly dragged a giggle from her in response.

She draped one arm over Gabel's shoulder and pressed to his chest. "Then you have nothing to be jealous of."

Gabel pressed teasing kisses to her lips.

"But we *are* going to the cen-centennial," she informed him, walking the fingers of her hand up his chest. "Davril will receive his blessing."

He nodded, his lips teasing at hers as his head moved up and down. "I will...contain my jealousy and not deprive either of you of the blessings the gods offer." He pressed his hands to her back, pulling Rostana to his body. "Am I forgiven?"

"For trying to protect me?" What an odd idea? How could any woman be angry at her husband for so noble a goal?

"Yes."

"As long as you promise not to keep such secrets from me again. I am your wife, after all."

Gabel groaned. He slid one hand to the edge of the shift she'd stripped to. His fingers explored beneath the edge and trailed along her inner thigh.

Rostana recognized the question and murmured her agreement.

Gabel glanced at their son. "Perhaps we should retire to the bedroom," he whispered.

She nodded. "We might wake him."

He lifted her into his arms and carried Rostana to the door. She lifted the latch and swung the door wide, then closed it softly behind them once they were outside.

Gabel made it from one room to the other in a hand of heartbeats, pushed the door — already ajar — open with his foot, and then kicked it shut. Rostana laughed, and he stopped to stare at her.

She didn't wait for him to voice his question. "It reminds me of our first night."

His eyes went hot in promise that made her heart stutter. "I believe that night may be worth repeating."

"Yes." Rostana gasped at his move toward the bed, certain that feeding Davril would be the only variation for them.

A completely sacrilegious thought flitted through her mind. *Kar is lacking. He will never match Gabel between the sheets.*

CHAPTER EIGHT

Rostana closed her eyes to the riot of color and movement, exhausted though she'd spent the last two hours in the lap of luxury.

The celebration arena at the royal temple in Aidalyn was decorated in banners of the He-Atal's red and the Ician's blue. Fire pots lit the far corners of the massive, domed space. Ice sculptures formed the line of separation between the mother's alcove and the general seating for other attendees.

Calling the area for new babes and their parents an alcove seemed somewhat disingenuous, since it held more than a hundred new families. Each young mother had been outfitted with a nursing lounge, each father with a comfortable chair and a footstool, and each babe with a lush cradle. Moreover, the area was hardly crowded; each family had been afforded space enough to rest in peace from each other. However, in comparison to the full arena, it was indeed a small enclosure within a much larger space.

There were easily ten thousand attendees in the outer rings of seating surrounding the mother's alcove. Though there were chairs for everyone invited — and even private boxes lining the entryway the Walking Gods would use, intended for nobles and royals — Rostana doubted anyone else in attendance were as pampered as the mothers and babes were.

There were buffets of food and drinks and even servants assigned to see to every comfort a mother or babe might require. There were stacks of cushions and blankets, scented oil pots, and priestess healers ready to handle the slightest complaint. Though bearing women and new mothers were always catered to, the cen-centennial put any other comforts shown them to shame.

Of course, that was tradition. Since the greatest blessing that could come of a centennial was a child between the He-Atal and the former Ician — now He-Atalia, it was believed the Walking Gods giving blessings to the new mothers and babes of the kingdom might bring such blessings upon the God-Couple themselves.

"Rostana?" Gabel whispered. He was most likely loath to wake her, if she'd fallen asleep as she had in the coach.

She opened her eyes to find him hovering over her. The light filtering through the huge windows was much darker than it had been when she'd closed her eyes. Had she slept again? It was possible. She'd slept poorly the night before.

"Would you like anything to eat before the celebration begins?" He was tense, and she didn't question what caused it.

Her own stomach was tied in knots as well. "Not at the moment. Perhaps a glass of juice, though?"

Gabel didn't have to make a move. At her query, the servant assigned to them bowed and rushed away to fulfill her request.

His shoulders tensed, and though Gabel didn't voice his concern, Rostana knew he was tapping down his unease at the idea of Kar touching her during the ceremony. She smiled at him and covered Gabel's hands with one of her own; he managed a smile in return.

A murmur stirred and rose. Clapping and cheers overpowered it.

Rostana stiffened in the realization that the Walking Gods must have arrived. She took a calming breath and looked toward the walkway.

Any secret hopes she might have harbored that Gabel was incorrect were squelched at the sight of Kar, arm in arm with a beautiful woman with straight, white hair and eyes of Ician blue. They were dressed in matching outfits. Kar wore tight trousers in his usual red, and the He-Atalia wore a matching sheath of a dress. Both were barefoot.

It was indecent. Both of them were. Their clothing was appropriate for the bedroom or one's own home, if their servants were tolerant sorts. Lir would most likely leave without a backward glance if she and Gabel acted so outrageously.

At least he's wearing more than I'm accustomed to seeing him clothed in. She bit back a wince at her relief that Kar wasn't wearing his waist wrap. Of course, her relief was for Gabel. Seeing the He-Atal in so immodest an outfit might have pushed her husband too far.

"Rostana?"

She turned to Gabel and accepted the cup of juice from him. After a sip, she thanked him.

His expression announced clearly that he was ill at ease. "Are you well?" he asked, glancing at the hovering servant out of the corner of his eyes.

Rostana pressed a kiss to his lips and smiled more naturally that time. "With you by my side, I could not be unwell."

He nodded solemnly.

* * * *

The He-Atal started his rounds of blessings on the far side of the ring, moving in a counter-clockwise direction. Gabel was relieved that he had time to compose himself at the same time he wished for this blasted event to be done with.

Rostana seemed calm, by comparison. His enchanting young bride wiped the leavings of their son's latest meal from his face, crooning to him.

She glanced up at Gabel, her smile wide and her eyes bright. Now that Rostana had recovered from the trip, she was alert.

Gabel conceded that he would prefer her to be asleep when the He-Atal approached them.

No. This is a once in a lifetime event. She deserves to see our son receive the Walking Gods' blessing.

The entire situation was maddening. Her reaction to the He-Atal had indicated Rostana had no interest past a purely academic one in the young God Vessel. That should have put Gabel's mind at ease, but the certainty that Rostana was trying to hide her own unease at Karliss Furia's proximity was impossible for him to shake free.

The Walking Gods approached, making their way through blessing after blessing.

Perhaps he will be so jaded by the time he reaches us, he will fail to notice Rostana. It was possible. After all, the He-Atal had surely had hundreds of women in his time.

A glance at Rostana confirmed that he was deluding himself. No matter how many women a man met or bedded, one like Rostana would be impossible to forget.

Gabel was so lost in his conflicting thoughts, he didn't note the approaching company until a deep voice rumbled out.

"Lady Tiben, how nice to meet you again."

He snapped a look up, prepared to question how the He-Atal had known Rostana's new name. He couldn't possibly know every councilor, and Gabel knew well that he'd only met the young prince once, long before he left for his training in Magmalen. Did he have people reporting on his former lovers? Or at least the ones he'd been most taken with?

The sight of the Walking God executing a formal bow the likes of one Gabel would offer the king stilled his tongue. The He-Atalia bowed her head as well.

His head spun. It wasn't a greeting either had offered the other families. Was there meaning in it?

"And you," Rostana offered in what he was sure was a falsely cordial voice, her back stiff as if in military review.

Karliss turned toward Gabel and offered his hand. "And you, Lord Tiben. It has been many years."

He accepted the handshake, confused by this turn of events. "It has indeed."

The He-Atal's hand was warm, despite the chill in the air, but not uncomfortably so.

The He-Atalia leaned over and tickled Davril's cheek, prompting a spate of manic movement from the babe. "What an adorable child," she breathed.

Karliss smiled and turned toward Rostana. He placed a hand on Davril's forehead, retreated, and did the same to Rostana. "May you gift your husband with many strong children."

The He-Atalia placed a kiss where Karliss had touched. "A long and happy life," she blessed them.

The Walking Gods offered one final nod and smile for Gabel and moved along.

In the stillness after their departure, Gabel found himself at a loss for words and strangely calm.

Rostana shifted Davril on her lap, and Gabel rushed to help her.

For a moment, she stared at him. There were many questions Gabel wanted to ask, but all fought emerging.

"I felt nothing for him," she informed him. "He is...an old acquaintance and nothing more."

Gabel pressed a kiss to her lips. "I am glad to hear it."

A wicked little smiled curved her lips, and her eyes glittered in mischief. "I do feel something, though."

"For me?" he chanced asking.

She leaned close to him and breathed her answer against his ear. "When Davril is older and I am fully recovered..."

His heart stuttered in the certainty that whatever she was about to suggest was sexual in nature. "Yes, Rostana?"

She pulled back and met his eyes fully, her expression full of promise. "I believe we are lacking a daughter to spoil."

Gabel captured her lips in a searing kiss, the heat rising between them. "As soon as the gods allow."

* * * *

"Is there a problem, Kar?"

He peeled his gaze from Rostana and her husband — locked in a kiss that spoke of Magmon's hunger — and focused on Diama. "Not at all."

Rostana has found her happiness. That is good. Though it wasn't what she'd come to Magmalen to find, Rostana's life was a blessed one. One Kar hoped he and Diama would be gifted themselves.

"Who is she?" Diama asked.

Her interest seemed sincere. "An acquaintance from long ago. She appeared at the temple in Magmalen, a traveler from the north, in need of counsel."

"And did you help her?"

Kar glanced at the couple again, noting her coy smile for her husband. Her cheeks were flushed, and her eyes spoke of sensual plans. "I believe I might have. I hope I did."

If any of her happiness is my doing, I am glad I was able to help.

ABOUT THE AUTHOR

Brenna Lyons wears many hats, sometimes all on the same day: former president of EPIC, author of more than 100 published works, owner of Fireborn Publishing, columnist, special needs teacher, wife, mother...and member in good standing of more than 60 writing advocacy groups.

In her first ten years published in novel-length, she's won 3 EPIC e-Book Awards (out of 15 finalists) and finaled for 3 PEARLS (including one Honorable Mention, second to NY Times Bestseller Angela Knight), 2 CAPAS, and a Dream Realm Award. She's also taken Spinetingler's Book of the Year for 2007.

Brenna writes in 26 established worlds plus stand-alones, poetry, articles and essays. She's a bestseller in indie/e fantasy and horror, straight genre and cross-genres thereof. Brenna has been termed "one of the most deviant erotic minds in the publishing world...not for the weak." (Rachelle for Fallen Angels Reviews) Milieu-heavy dark work is practically Brenna's calling card, with or without the erotic content.

She teaches classes in everything from POV studies to advanced editing, networking to marketing. Brenna enjoys hearing from people who read her work and can be reached by e-mail.

Website: http://www.brennalyons.com/

Facebook: http://www.facebook.com/brenna.lyons

Email: brennalyons4168@live.com

ALSO BY THIS AUTHOR

Available from *Fireborn Publishing*

KEIF'S DEN AND PACK
Keif's Pack
Mother of the Keif
Keif's Den (Coming Soon)

PROPHECY
Prophecy: Revelations
Prophecy: Rapture
The Prophet's Mate
Prophecy: Rampage - Meet Gavin
Prophecy: Rampage (Coming Soon)

THE FANTASY CLUB
The Consort

Beyond the Veil
Fairy Wishes (Coming Soon)
Mine for the Night
Once in a Blue Moon
Overtime Pay
Stay With Me
The Fire God's Woman
The Punishment of Phoebus Apollo
Werewolf U

Available from *Phaze Books*

ANGEL-WING SAGA
Sons of Heaven: Beldon
Daughters of Man: Prize Match
Sons of Heaven: Unexpected Mates
Daughters of Man: Claiming a Princess

BRIDE BALL
Bride Ball
Poison, Lies, and No-Win Choices

COLOR OF LOVE
The Color of Love

FIRE AND ICE
Magmon's Hunger
Magmon's Lover

INSTINCT SERIES
Animal Instincts

KEGIN SERIES
Conquest
The Last of Fion's Daughters
Last Chance for Love
Rites of Mating
In Her Ladyship's Service
Matchmaker's Misery

KIELAN SERIES
The Lady's Lowborn Lover
Time Currents
Cubed

NIGHT WARRIORS
Night Warriors
Will of the Stone
Bearing Armen
Hunter's Moon
Maher Men
Choosing a Mate/Starting a War
Raised to Be His Own
Veriel's Tales I: Crossbearer Turned
Veriel's Tales II: Losing Regana
Blutjagdfrau Lost
The Warrior's Man
Damsel in Distress

STAR MAGES
The Master's Lover

XXAN WAR
Daahan Rising
Crossbred Son
Raashh Decisions

Enslaved
All I Want for Christmas is You
Fates Magic
All's Fair…
Black Sail
Mama's Tales
Dream Walk
Unexpected Daddy
Phaze in Verse
We Shall Live Again
May the Best Man Win
Nevermore
Marked
And It Was Good

Available from **Mundania Press**

STAR MAGES
Written in the Stars

Fairy Dreams
Monsters of Myth Anthology

Available from **Under the Moon**

RENEGADES SERIES
TYGERS
Renegade's Run
Max Sec

URBAN GRIMM
Catch Me, If You Can
Three Wishes
Temptation of Eve

With Great Power
Undead in Blue
Evil Overlords Union Issue #1 Anthology
Undead Embrace
"Playing Games" in *Forbidden Love: Bad Boys*
"Marked" in *Forbidden Love: Wicked Women*
"The Master's Lover" in *Forbidden Love: Sacred Bands*

Available from ***Logical Lust***

"Mine for the Night" in *The Cougar Book* Anthology

Available from ***Coming Together Charity Anthologies***

INSTINCT SERIES
"Foundling" in *Coming Together: Into the Light* Anthology

"Claim Mate" (available separately and as part of the *Coming Together: Against the Odds* Anthology)
"The Fire God's Woman" in *Coming Together: Under Fire* Anthology

Available ***self-published***

KEGIN SERIES
Earth-Born Lord
Graham: Training the Earth-Born Lord

NIGHT WARRIORS
Claiming a Lady
Stone Lord

Mother's Son

COLOR OF LOVE
A Safe Heart

Snapshots from a Poet's Life

AWARD WINNING BOOKS

EPPIE/EPIC eBOOK AWARDS WINNERS
Coming Together: Against the Odds- 2010
Time Currents- 2010
Coming Together: Into the Light- 2011

EPPIE/EPIC eBOOK AWARDS FINALISTS
Fion's Daughter- 2004
Collected Poems: Book One- 2005 (now titled *Snapshots of a Poet's Life*)
Renegade's Run- 2005
Rites of Mating- 2006
All I Want for Christmas- 2006
Phaze in Verse- 2008
"The Fire God's Woman" in Coming Together: Under Fire- 2009
Three Wishes- 2010
Matchmaker's Misery- 2010
The Cougar Book- 2011
The Master's Lover- 2011
Bride Ball- 2011

DREAM REALM AWARDS FINALIST
Last Chance for Love- 2003

PEARL HONORABLE MENTION
Night Warriors- 2004

PEARL FINALISTS
Schente Night- 2003 (now included in *The Last of Fion's Daughters*)
König Cursebreakers- 2004 (now titled *Will of the Stone*)

JOYFULLY REVIEWED BEST BOOKS OF 2010
Written in the Stars- 2010

SPINETINGLER'S BOOK OF THE YEAR 2007
NOBODY: An Anthology of Dark Fiction- 2007 (Brenna's pieces
of the anthology can be found in *Beyond the Veil*)

TRS's CAPA FINALISTS
Ultimate Warriors- 2004 (Brenna's portion is now available as
With Great Power)
Written in the Stars

LOVE ROMANCE AND MORE CAFÉ BOOK OF THE YEAR
RUNNER UP
Last Chance for Love- 2008

ROAD TO ROMANCE REVIEWERS' CHOICE AWARD
Prophecy: Revelations- 2004

LOVE ROMANCES REVIEWERS' CHOICE AWARD
Black Sail- 2003

ROMANCE JUNKIES BOOK CLUB STAFF PICK
TYGERS- 2003

FALLEN ANGELS ROMANCE RECOMMENDED READ
*Devon's Price-*2005 (now available in *Bearing Armen*)

JOYFULLY RECOMMENDED READ
Fairy Dreams- 2008
The Last of Fion's Daughters- 2009

TREBLE HEART FINALIST
Prophecy: Revelations- 2003

www.ingramcontent.com/pod-product-compliance
Lightning Source LLC
Chambersburg PA
CBHW050019180626
46810CB00002B/486